MA-JI

MA-JI

Seer of Ages

A novel

Byron Dye

Library of Congress Number: 2004095156
ISBN: Hardcover   1-4134-6351-7
                Softcover   1-4134-6350-9

This book was printed in the United States of America.

To order additional copies of this book, contact:
Xlibris Corporation
1-888-795-4274
www.Xlibris.com
Orders@Xlibris.com
25401

CONTENTS

. . . To Randy, without whose help the photograph on the cover would never have been taken.

. . . To Kolt . . . for all the memories never made; always you will be with us and always we will be but a moment away. Nothing can separate love, for death is but the cord that binds life together.

. . . To Rita, thank you for all the times you let me drone on-and-on about my writing, you always made me feel that you enjoyed hearing about it just as much as I enjoyed the telling of it . . . just keep swimming!

. . . And lastly, for my parents (M.C. and Ina) who never stopped believing that I could be anything that I wanted to be . . . forever grateful, your son!

CHAPTER 1

A New Home

A black cloud had loomed over our country—for the last eleven years—since a failed revolt had left us with a puppet king. Now revolt was in the air again, and it was only a matter of time before, like a large locust invasion, they would come, devouring everything. But since I was only fifteen, my life was focused on the more immediate needs of my village—the harvest. All other able-bodied men had been sent to the country's border to meet the armies of the East.

My name, by the way, is Daniel, and I lived in a fertile valley by the name of Thelema. We enjoyed a simple life and made our living in the fields. My two older sisters, Berea and Doma, cared for the household chores while Father and I joined the rest of the villagers to harvest the grain. Mother had not been well since she had fallen sick of fever the previous spring. She never seemed to fully regain all her strength.

I remember that the weather had been dry and hot that season—good for drying the grain husks but hard on the backs of all the workers. We would sweat our clothes through before the sun was even halfway into the sky; our necks were burned; and our hands were worn to blisters with grasping the sickle.

My tale starts on a dry sun-scorched day . . .

It was just before noon when it happened. Father was the first to notice the dust swelling into the air, a sure sign that many riders on horseback were headed in our direction. We scarcely had time to make our way out to the edges of the field before they were upon us.

Father pushed me back into the high stalks of grain before the riders could grasp how many of us there were. "Kill all those who resist," cried one of the guards. "Burn all the fields, let none escape."

My father and the others were rounded up and carried away before I could do anything to help them. My only choice was to move farther into the field to avoid detection, but then the unthinkable—fire! There were torches being thrown in all directions. I had no recourse but to run before the fire and smoke overtook me. Maybe they wouldn't see me through the thick smoke. I was wrong.

I could feel the earth thunder as a rider swooped down upon me like some bird of prey. With all my might I fought him, knocking both of us to the ground. But I was no match for him. He was twice my size and skilled in battle. Before I knew what had happened, he had drawn his sword and was preparing to strike.

"Halt," cried a guard who appeared suddenly out of the smoke. "Save this one for Ashpenaz. He shows the cunning of a fox and may be of value."

"Who was that man?" I asked as the other rider rode away.

"That was Arioch, captain of the King's Guard. You owe your life to him," replied the guard as he re-sheathed his sword.

As sure as I had thought that my life was over, at the last possible moment, it had turned. I saw my father and the others being led away toward the village, but I, exhausted and filthy, I alone was carried away. The rest of the captain's guards continued their campaign through the countryside. Only one broke ranks to carry me to the court of Ashpenaz, which would be held in our ruling city, Axios. We rode hard on one horse for two full days before entering the city.

I had been there during the yearly feasts (but then only to the markets of the peasants), but this time, I was being carried right into the heart of the city, to the very palace itself. Such majesty and beauty I never knew existed except in the stars at night. The palace stood at the top of a multitude of stairs, stairs which seemed to surround the entire building so that no matter how one entered, it would have to be up this royal stairway.

Pillars flanked all sides of this building and held up an enormous portico. There were many soldiers around, and inside, there seemed to be hundreds of people waiting. For what? I did not ask. The Captain's Guard escorted me into a grand hallway and presented me to Menou, a eunuch and overseer of all newly arriving charges. It was his job to make all who came to him presentable before the master of the eunuchs, Ashpenaz.

Before I could ask the first question, I was whisked away and a dozen hands were removing my filthy clothes and submerging me into a hot bath of some pungent aroma. It was so strong that it made me sneeze. From there, I was clothed in a soft linen robe and led to another chamber where one person worked on my fingernails, another was doing something to my feet, and still another was hacking away at my hair.

In yet another chamber, I found myself standing on some sort of stool, being measured from head to toe. The finest material was draped and pinned to every inch of my body. And as quickly as they had come (the cobblers and the seamstresses), they were gone.

"All will be ready tomorrow," they said as they bowed themselves out of the room.

I was taken back to Menou who hardly recognized me.

"Yes, yes," he said. "I would be very surprised indeed if you are not one of the chosen."

"Chosen . . . chosen for what?" I said, before I had thought better of it.

"Oh, that's right. I forget that you, being from the countryside, are not aware of the king's order," Menou mused as we walked along darkened corridors toward the sleeping chambers. "All those in whom is found no flaw, are skillful in wisdom, cunning in knowledge, and are suitable to stand before the king of Babylon, are to be chosen for training in his special courts," said Menou.

"Tomorrow, you, along with others of your kingdom, will be brought before Ashpenaz to be judged by his court. Those chosen will leave immediately for that city of cities, that emerald of the desert—Babylon." He said all this in the most wistful way. "But tonight, you must rest with the others. Your chambers are here. I will come for you all in the morning. Rest well."

And with that, Menou took his leave of me, and I entered the darkened chambers. Since I had arrived so late in the day, I wasn't able to join the others before they had been settled in for the night.

"Hey, watch it!" someone called as I tripped over what felt like a large sack of potatoes lying on the floor.

"I'm sorry. I didn't see you there," I said. "As a matter of fact, I can't see much of anything in here."

"You must be new," said another voice coming from a higher vantage point.

"My name is Daniel," I said, talking to the darkness. "I'm from the valley of Thelema in the south."

Suddenly a lamplight appeared, scattering the darkness, and I could just barely make out the outlines of many makeshift beds thrown on the floor or wherever there was room.

"My name is Hananiah, but my friends call me Hanan," said the boy that I had tripped over. "And this is e-Shack and Abed. We are from the northern provinces here to study in the king's court. I have been here the longest and am head of my class," Hanan relayed proudly. "Abed and e-Shack arrived only one year ago. Are you here to stand before the court of Ashpenaz tomorrow as well?"

"Yes," I said uncertainly, "but I don't know why they brought me here. Who is Ashpenaz? And what do they want with us?"

"The word is," began Abed, "that we are to be judged by our ever-wise captors in order to find those who will be able to stand before the great king of Babylon and be added to his already-overgrown ego."

"What happens to those who are not chosen?" I reflected.

"No one knows," said e-Shack. "But one thing is for sure: If we don't get some sleep, we won't be awake to find out if we are chosen or not. Let's get some shut-eye. Daniel, you can bed down over here by me. Lights out!"

Not another sound was uttered. As I lay there in the darkness, I couldn't help but wonder what this night was like for my family so far away. Were they comforted as I was, or were they being abused and tormented by our stern, new masters? I think that I could have easily guessed the answer to that one, however.

The next morning, we were awakened early and led away to a sumptuous breakfast. Anything that you could think of to eat was there—all manner of fowl and beast of the field and different kinds of fruit that had never been seen in my part of the kingdom before. I wasn't very hungry and only ate that which I knew had come from the fields of my own land.

Hanan was busy telling everyone that would listen about all the various types of fruit that was set before us, reciting what their names were and where they had come from. It seemed that he had gone through several classes on such things.

After breakfast, we were all taken to different chambers and fitted with our newly sewn garments. And what garments these were. Such rich colors I could not even have imagined existed. And the fabric was so smooth to the touch. There were pants of a tan color with white linen shirts and a red and gold vest that was to be pulled over the head and tied around the waist with golden ropes. The vest hung from the shoulders midway to the knee, and there was much murmuring that some parts of the cloth had been sown with thread made from real gold.

Finally, dressed and groomed, the lot of us was led to the great hall. There we were formed into one single line that started from the great doors and wound around the pillars of the inner courtyard. At least one hundred of us waited to be brought, one by one, before the court of Ashpenaz.

Some were taken in and out quickly, while others remained for a much longer period. Some did not return to the great hall at all. Since leaving the dressing chambers, I lost contact with the others that I had met the night before. I did see e-Shack some twenty people behind me, but the lines wound so through the corridors that I could not locate either Hanan or Abed. No one was allowed to talk or to leave the line once it was formed.

Slowly I moved closer and closer to the front of the line. Finally, I was standing before the guard posted at the door to the court. My heart strained at the thought of what was about to happen. I still didn't know if I wanted to be chosen or not. Would I be sent back to my family? Or would I just end up a prisoner in the city?

As my mind raced with the possibilities, the door opened yet again. The one who had entered just ahead of me was now exiting with his head bowed low, and in great distress. Now, the grand doors opened for me.

I followed the guard into a hallway just inside the door. There I was met by Menou once again. He smiled a pleasant smile and led me toward a room up ahead. "Just be yourself and answer all questions with a thoughtful response," he said in a hushed tone.

And the next moment, I stood before the court of Ashpenaz.

The room was rectangular, and immense pillars stood behind a golden throne. Colorful tapestries adorned the walls, and light flooded the room through shuttered windows that had been thrown open to receive the dawn. As I stepped forward into the chamber, I noticed two others bearing writing scrolls and pens. They murmured to each other in some unfamiliar language.

"Step forward and give us your name," commanded Ashpenaz.

"My name is Daniel of Thelema," I said.

The scribes pored over their scrolls trying to find any record, but quickly looked up at Ashpenaz and shook their heads.

"Who brought you here?" inquired Ashpenaz.

"I was taken by Arioch in the grain fields of my homeland while trying to escape," I explained curtly.

"Bravery against enormous odds," he mused, "or the greatest stupidity at thinking that you could actually escape. And what have you of learning and understanding science?" Ashpenaz continued.

"My father taught me how to navigate by the night sky and to know when to plant the crops and when to harvest. He taught me how to talk to the land and how to hear its answer, how to find water in a baron wasteland, how to become invisible to the eyes of the enemy," I answered.

"And yet here you are, captured," Ashpenaz interjected. "You speak of such cunning. So how do you explain that?"

"I would have been able to escape if the captain's guards hadn't thought of burning the fields from both ends at once, trapping me in the middle. I still would have escaped if it hadn't been for one guard who spotted me through the smoke. He was about to kill me when Arioch stopped him and ordered that I should be sent to you," I further explained.

"Arioch has a keen eye that I trust. You are small of stature but with a good head about you. The king's table will fatten you up, and you seem pliable enough to learn what we shall teach you." Ashpenaz had found a liking for my feistiness, I suppose, and with a smile, he turned to the scribes and proclaimed, "Add this one to the list of agricultural knowledge."

I was led away into a different chamber where stood six others. Only one turned his head as I entered.

"So, you've been chosen as well," he said gloomily.

"What happens now," I asked. And the boy who stood before me simply shrugged his shoulders.

We all sat around in silence waiting for the court of Ashpenaz to conclude. After what seemed like an eternity, we were all asked to return to the great hall to be told who would be leaving on the journey to the great city of the East. There were different groups standing separately in the hallway, but one thing was for sure: now, there were only about thirty of us left.

Ashpenaz came into the room through the main doors that we had all ourselves entered to his court. The room grew quiet as he began to speak: "You have been reviewed by my court and found promising in your various abilities. I have separated you out by current levels of achievement and to aid in your placement once you arrive in the halls of Babylon. All others have been returned to their previous states and have taken their leave of us. Tonight, rest well for tomorrow, we begin a great journey. Congratulations to you all!" said Ashpenaz. And then he was gone.

To my great surprise, Hanan, e-Shack, and Abed had all been selected into another group. We spent the next few hours catching up on what each had been asked when they too stood before Ashpenaz.

The rest of the day brought more preparation for the journey we were about to begin. Hanan was more impressed with himself than ever before and made a great deal out of every detail. We had our last look at Axios and made our way to the sleep chambers once again. This time, there was plenty of room for all to sleep comfortably.

The next morning was about as much fun as a toothache. We were pulled here and there and hurried through breakfast in order to get an early start. Servants were scurrying to make last-minute changes to the caravan. Our job was easy—just to wait. But I would rather work anytime than to stand around. Finally, Menou came for us. We were dressed in our royal raiment and led from the great hall to the northern portico. What met our eyes set off a storm of excited murmuring among the groups—horses, thirty white horses in five rows of six abreast. They were adorned with the most exquisite saddles and blankets of red and gold. Tassels hung from the reins, and leather covered the faces of each horse so that only the eyes and the nose were visible.

"Select a horse and mount from the left side, please," Menou instructed, and the crowd moved toward the horses as they pawed and snorted into the wind.

Hanan, Abed, e-Shack, and I took four horses together in the middle of the procession. Abed had some difficulty in gaining his mount as he had never before ridden a horse. The horse seemed to sense that.

The whole city had turned out to watch the procession as it made its way through the main thoroughfare and out the eastern gate. Many wept as they watched us being carried away, captives into a foreign land.

We were both led and trailed by a host of the captain's guards and Arioch himself directed the forces. Menou was behind us with the caravan of wagons filled with the provisions that we would need on our journey. Ashpenaz was not to be seen, however. I wondered if he had gone on ahead, or if he had other business in Axios.

Our first day's journey brought us to the easternmost border of our country. On a sheltered portion of a hillside, we made our camp. Most complained sorely about the rigors of being horse-bound for the last eleven hours. I was just happy to be on solid ground once again. The Captain's Guard took posts along the ridge above our encampment and we were put up in tents, which were completely surrounded by other guards. Since the guards all dressed in black, they would appear and disappear into the cold night air without warning.

Campfires began to blaze, and the day's dirt was bathed away. Fresh clothes and plenty of liquid seemed to take some of the pain out of the backsides.

Abed looked as if he would be permanently bowlegged, and Hanan had run out of interesting things to comment about, so e-Shack and I decided to go for a walk to see if we could coax our legs back into operation. As we staggered unevenly along the sandy soil, we were suddenly startled by a rambunctious verbal exchange taking place over to our left. Upon further investigation, we encountered several guards engaged in conversation about some dreams that they had had the night before.

"I don't know anything about what it means," one began, "but I remember seeing a huge silo filled with grain, so much so that it overflowed the top and ran out onto the ground. Flowers began to bloom all over the hillside, and a great house appeared on the horizon. It was covered with ivy and made of stone from its foundation to its uppermost stories, and there were three stories.

"The first story and second story had flower boxes of some pink flower, and the third story was adorned in the most striking sky blue for its flower boxes. In the doorway stood my wife, and she beckoned me to come, then I woke up."

"Awe, that's nothing," said another guard, anxious to tell his dream. "My dream is a real man's dream. I was in a dark city, walking through muddied streets, when I happened upon a gambling house and decided to stop in. Well, three others were there sitting at a card table, as if waiting for something. They invited me to join them for a simple game of high card, winner takes all. The table was overflowing with golden coins. And since none of them looked bright enough to come in out of the rain, I threw my coins into the pot.

"The cards were cut, and each reached over the deck to take the next card. The man to my left began, so that I was the last to draw. With all the cards already on the table, I reached for the last card. In picking up just the corner, I realized that it would not beat the cards already laid down, so I created a distraction and selected the second card down instead. No one noticed. I was the winner and took all the gold and filled my pockets and my hat and walked from the room, chuckling to myself. But the funny part is that on my way back to camp, it began to rain, and the gold coins dissolved into pools of mud, and blood ran down my face to my feet."

Upon hearing this, it became clear to me what the dreams meant. I had once told a traveler to our village what his dream meant but did not find out until one year later that I had been correct. My father, from then on, had told me to be discreet about this great gift. But somehow, being so far from home and not knowing these men, I felt that I could perhaps help without anyone taking too much notice.

"Sirs," I said. "I do not mean to pry or to insert myself wrongly into your private affairs. However, I believe that I can interpret the meaning of the dreams that you have recounted."

The first man asked, "You are from the captives of Axios, are you not?"

"Yes," I replied cautiously.

"Perhaps there is something that you could add to our understanding of these matters," he continued.

"Oh, please," the other objected, "these are but children, and what would they know of the world?"

"Well, I for one would like to hear what they have to say. What harm can it do?" added the first guard. "So what do you think?"

I walked over to the first guard, sat down beside him, and began to recount the different portions of his dream.

"First," I said, "you spoke of a great silo filled to overflowing with grain."

"Yes, that's right," the first guard agreed.

"This means that you will be greatly blessed of the land with much to eat for many years. The second part was about the hillside covered with flowers and a great house on the horizon. This means that you will be blessed of the womb. The house with its three stories reveals that you will have two daughters and one son, all strong and able-bodied like the stone. Your wife beckoning means that you must decide between the guard and the family. Choose wisely!"

And the first guard smiled and walked away in a blissful daze. The second guard, encouraged by the favorable interpretation that had just been given, decided to try his luck.

"Well, I still think that this is all a bunch of rubbish," he moaned, "but why not? It's all in fun, right? Go ahead and tell me what my dream means."

I turned toward the second guard and noticed that a crowd had begun to gather, eagerly awaiting the second interpretation.

"As I recall," I began, "your dream started with the darkened streets of a city. You entered along a muddy street and found yourself in front of a gambling establishment."

"Yeah," the second guard grunted.

"You entered into a room with three men seated 'round a card table. The table was piled high with gold coins and they asked you to join them for a game of high card. You did, and won the game by cheating. After loading your pockets with the gold, you left to return to the encampment and found that the gold coins had turned to mud and that your head was covered in blood. Is this correct?" I asked.

"Yeah, that's about the size of it. So what does it mean? Am I going to be rich?" asked the second guard, impatiently.

"The interpretation," I cautioned, "is not a pleasant one. In three days' time, you will enter a town of wanton reputation and find there a game of chance that will provide you no luck. You, however, confident of the outcome, will engage in this game with treachery in your heart and with your winnings in hand will be struck down by bandits in the street."

"What are you saying?" demanded the second guard in a rage. "Do you honestly think that a mighty warrior like myself is going to be struck down by some two-bit street bandits when I have been twice decorated by the captain of the King's Guard himself." He turned to address his fellows, "Just as I said, rubbish." And he arose and stormed away. e-Shack and I thought it best to head back to our campfire before things turned too sour.

"I didn't know that you could interpret dreams," said e-Shack with a bit of surprise in his voice.

"Well, sometimes it's best to keep things secret," I explained. "I used to get a lot of people asking me to tell them what this meant and what that meant. Before long, it was all I ever heard. And people get mad at you when you tell them something bad is going to happen. They act like it's your fault somehow. I just give them the message from what I see," I said.

Fifteen minutes later, we arrived back into our own camp and began to make ready for our first night in the desert. As we retired to our tents, we caught sight of the guards located high on the hillside. There wouldn't be any sleep for them tonight. I felt sorry for them. They were going to be in for a long, grueling night. It is a most cruel punishment to be denied sleep, wonderful, marvelous sleep.

Maybe it was all the talk of dreams from the two guards that had set my mind to the subject, but that very night, I too was visited by a strange dream. In this dream, I was walking alone in the desert just below the crest of a hill. Upon reaching the top, I saw a great vista stretched out before me. I could see a caravan winding its way through the low-lying hills toward a remote settlement just beyond a river. The settlement was filled with men dressed in the usual country attire. The one exception, however, was that all their faces were covered by masks (ashen white masks), and their movements seemed contrived and unnatural.

Just then, the morning trumpet sounded the wake-up call. With the dream still fresh in my mind, I tried to make out what it might mean. Masks of ashen white always meant death to me. Did this mean that the village had been overtaken by disease and that we should stay away? But before I could think on the matter longer, we were starting to pack up and get a quick bite of breakfast. I could not consider the matter further at that time.

Soon we were on our way. Horseback didn't quite seem to have the allure that it had elicited just one day before, but be that as it may, it kept us above most of the dust that the many horse hooves kicked up.

As our journey into the land of Shinar continued, a rhythm began to develop. Each day became just a copy of the one before. One day, however, as the sunlight began to wane, we came upon the outskirts of a small city, the first real civilization that we had seen since leaving Axios. But before we could get our hopes up, we were informed that it was much too dangerous to allow us all to go into the city. Some guards, however, were given permission to take a short, well-earned rest stop.

All e-Shack, Hanan, Abed, and I could do was to sit in our encampment and watch the lights from a distance. We talked about what we would have done had we been able to scout the city. Abed was most interested in finding extra padding for his saddle. Hanan and I discussed at length the type of government that must surely be in place in a city such as this for it to be so well taken care of. We argued the merits of slave labor versus voluntary participation in the outcome of public projects. My head always hurt after these kinds of conversations.

"e-Shack," I said, as something finally became clear to me.

"Do you want some more fruit?" he replied

"No. I just finally realized what something meant," I mused. At that, both Abed and Hanan looked up as well.

"A few nights ago, I had a dream. I was walking alone in the desert when I came to the top of a small hill and noticed a caravan winding its way toward a river. On the opposite bank was a small village. The interesting thing was that all the inhabitants, although dressed properly, had faces that were ashen white and expressionless, like masks. I knew that the caravan represented us, and that the river meant some kind of barrier to our forward progress. At first, I thought that maybe the village was consumed by a plague and that we would die if we entered there.

"But now, it is clear what this means. The village is an ambush. I fear the normal inhabitants have been killed and warriors have taken their place. They knew that we would be coming this way and plan to attack once the guards enter the village."

"These are our enemies," whispered Abed. "Maybe God is showing you our deliverance."

"Why does it have to mean anything? Maybe it was just a dream," remarked Hanan.

"What are you going to do about it?" asked e-Shack.

"Even though these are our enemies, I cannot let them walk unaware into their own deaths," I said. "God has given us over to the Chaldeans for a purpose. I must go and try to warn them."

"And who is going to believe you?" Hanan yelled after me as I walked away.

I was soon joined by e-Shack who asked me where I was going to go first.

"I am going to try and find Arioch. Or maybe Menou will listen," I responded uncertainly.

"You there, what are you up to this time of night?" a guard's voice came from the darkness.

"We are tying to find Arioch. I must talk with him. It's urgent," I said.

"Your urgent business will have to wait until the morning. Arioch has been called into the city on another matter. And as I am sure that you both are aware, any complaint that you might have is to be taken up with Menou. You are not to waste the captain's time. Is that clear?" The guard instructed in a severe voice.

"But . . ." I objected.

"No buts," reiterated the guard as a few others took note of the conversation and moved closer so as to cut off any impending altercation.

But at that very moment, several riders came galloping back into camp. Arioch was at the lead, and one man was over the saddle of his horse and had been tied into position.

"Balak is dead," stated Arioch. "Post a heavy guard around the entire encampment tonight. We leave at first light." Then Arioch demanded, "Why are these charges out of their tents at this hour?"

"Sir, I was just escorting them back when you arrived," the guard explained.

"Wait a minute," exclaimed another guard. "I know these boys. A few days ago, we were all sitting around the

evening fire when we started to talk about dreams that we
had had, just for amusement, of course. And this one"—he
pointed straight at me—"he explained to us what these
dreams foretold of our future. My god, Balak was there,
and his dream was that he would win gold in a gambling
house but then be robbed and killed by bandits in three
days' time. That was three days ago."

Everyone looked shocked, except Arioch.

"So, have you dreamed up my death somehow?" he
inquired.

"No, sir. Please give me just a moment to explain," I
implored.

"All right, you've got five minutes—in here." And he
pointed toward a nearby tent.

"Sir," I began awkwardly, "my . . . my dream was of a
caravan making its way through the low country when it
came upon . . . upon a river. On the other side of the river
was a small village. There were wooden platforms on both
sides of the river with ropes connecting the two. But there
was something strange about the villagers—they were not
as they should be. Their faces were covered in white ashen
masks, and they seemed to busy themselves awaiting some
event. I believe that their plan is to ambush your guards
and to take the caravan."

Arioch sat silent and motionless, staring into the canvas
walls of the tent. He sat there for a great length of time
before responding. I was sure that he would not believe us,
even after what he had just witnessed.

"In less than one day's time, we come to a river with a
small settlement on the eastern shores. It is a place for us to
clean up and refill our water supplies. You have described
it perfectly, and yet you have never been there. I will send a
scout forward to check out our approach," Arioch recited,
more thinking out loud than speaking.

"You two need to get back to your camp and get some
rest," Arioch commanded as he arose to show us from the tent.

We walked back to our camp with a guard. I was unsure if he did not trust us to return on our own, or if, perhaps, he was concerned with our safety. In any case, we talked in our own language as we returned so as to hide our conversation from the guard.

"Do you think that he believed us?" asked e-Shack.

"I don't know," I said. "Let's get some sleep and pray that we aren't heading for disaster tomorrow. We've done all we can; it's up to Arioch now."

"What do you think he'll do?" e-Shack added.

"He's the military genius. We'll just have to trust him," I responded.

We awoke just before dawn the next morning and found the encampment alive with activity. We packed up quickly and set off. We were only about an hour's ride to the river. Our approach had been carefully planned. Just before we came within sight of the village, we stopped and several of the guards exchanged their black horses for white ones. They were stripped down to only a bridle—no saddle, no blanket, nothing. The guards had also changed their normal black attire for white robes and headdress. Arioch came to the riders, spoke quietly to them, and directed them off toward the south.

Four of the provision carts had been moved to the front of the caravan. All manner of goods were being thrown out the back of each. Once emptied, the carts were filled with, of all things, guards. I saw four or five guards climb into each cart and cover themselves with cloth and bags of wheat. On the front seat, which usually was occupied by a woman, I saw the strangest sight of all: instead of the women driving the carts, guards were attempting to take their places. I could only hope that the bandits that awaited them across the river were half blind because these guys made the ugliest women you could imagine.

At this point, Menou had become quite interested in what was going on for, you see, he was responsible for the provisions and the carts. "Arioch? What is the meaning of this?" Menou protested.

"We have scouted the weigh station across the river," Arioch began, "and have reason to believe that bandits have overtaken the village and lie in wait to ambush us once we are ferried across."

"So what are we going to do?" Menou inquired, his voice cracking slightly.

"Well, this is the only place for us to ferry the carts across for a hundred sarons," Arioch continued, "and so, I have decided to just give them what they want—carts full of provisions."

"But . . . but . . . but . . ." Menou stammered.

Arioch smiled a mischievous smile, mounted his horse, and turned to ride away. "Look after the charges," he yelled back as he galloped out of sight.

He left a small complement of guards with the unloaded provisions and hastily led the caravan forward once more. As we rounded the bend, the hillside fell away revealing the river and a small village just on the other side. A rope was strung across the water to a platform on our side. A large wooden ferry was moored to a similar platform on the other side.

As far as the caravan was concerned, everything was as it should be. Well, almost. It was kind of hard to explain why all those provisions had just been dumped, but most people just took what came and didn't ask many questions.

Arioch rode to the shoreline ahead of everyone else and cast his gaze across the river. Things looked normal enough, and when he caught the ferryman's eye, he gave the appropriate signal. The ferryman returned the proper counter signal and released the lock on the ferry. Arioch's guards began to draw the ferry across the river by turning a large pulley mechanism. The men grunted and groaned as the ferry slowly made its way to the opposite shore.

Once firmly locked into place, four carts and just a couple guards were loaded from the platform onto the ferry. All in place, Arioch again signaled to the village ferryman. Now it was their turn to pull the ferry back. The men on the opposite shore struggled and groaned as they worked the pulley mechanism to return the ferry to their waiting clutches. They must have thought that they had hit it big as heavy as these carts were. And with only two guards and a few women to fight, life couldn't get any better. They would lock the ferry down on their side once it landed, steal the carts, and be gone before the guards could even attempt to swim the river and free up the ferry once more.

As the ferry came near to dock with the landing platform, all our eyes were focused on the opposite shore. The fighting broke out almost immediately. Additional bandits rushed from hiding places all around the dock area and stormed the landing. The two guards were overpowered and thrown into the water, and apparently, the women, too ugly to be kept, met the same fate. Happy with their ease of victory, some unsavory slurs were yelled in our general direction. But not a soul stirred from our side as Arioch held up his hand for us to hold our peace.

The bandits quickly moved the carts from the ferry onto solid ground, and with no further delay, headed east, out of the village and into the sunrise. They knew that it wouldn't take Arioch that long to get a couple dozen of his guards across the river and chase them down. They needed all the time they could get.

But Arioch had already taken this issue into consideration. The bandits, expediting their escape, ran straight into a band of white riders upon white horses, and with the sun shining into the bandit's eyes, these riders must have looked like the host of heaven. The carts came to an abrupt halt, whereupon the hidden cargo jumped out and stopped the unsuspecting bandits in their tracks.

When they all had arrived back in the village, the few guards that had come over on the first ferry were already docking the second ferry load to the platform. This load contained Arioch and fifteen of his mounted guards.

From our side, I could see that Arioch was making some comments to the bandit's leader. And with a wave of his hand, they were being led away to a building where they would probably be held until they could be delivered to a magistrate.

Hanan, e-Shack, Abed, and I were on the third ferry to cross the river. I was relieved to find out that the villagers had not been killed, just tied up. I could see some of them being brought to the dock area to talk with Arioch.

We could hear Arioch explain to the village leaders about how he had found out about the plot. It seemed that he had wanted the bandits to think that they had gotten away with stealing the carts from the ferry. This way, all the bandits would leave the village and then could be captured in an open area away from the villagers. He had sent the guards on white horses to cross the river to the south so they could forestall the bandits' escape. He hoped that the morning sun, coupled with the white horses and horsemen, would blind them to their existence until it was too late. He was right.

As Arioch finished with the elders, he glanced over his shoulder (as if knowing that I had been there all along), and with a small salute, he expressed his gratitude before riding off.

"Well," said e-Shack, "you certainly made a believer out of him."

"What are you two talking about?" Hanan interrupted. "Why doesn't anybody ever tell me anything? Why am I always the last to know?"

"If you would take a break from those scrolls every now and then," remarked Abed, "you might know." And with that, the four of us headed for the largest building we could find, and hopefully, a little less excitement for a change.

The rest of the day was filled with replenishing our water supplies and a well-deserved break from the journey. The villagers were throwing a huge makeshift party to show their gratitude for being rescued from the bandits. For, you see, the bandits had not been remiss in forgetting to rob the villagers of all their valuables as well.

Hanan rarely missed an opportunity to quiz us on basic Chaldean. He knew at least four other languages and made every effort to show us how much more he knew about this new language than we did. Menou had encouraged Hanan on this matter, so we decided not to fight it too much. Besides, it had already come in handy when dealing with the guards.

We had found a large round table off to one side of a bar packed with revelers, and settled in to practice writing. It seemed less like homework with everyone else around. We had just started conjugating irregular verbs when a commotion drew our attention to the front door.

All we could see was what looked like the top half of a walking stick beating and pushing its way through the crowd. As the crowd finally gave way, a small wisp of a woman, barely five feet tall, stood before us. She looked older than anyone that I had ever seen before. Wrinkles upon wrinkles covered her face and hands. On her head, she wore a torn shawl partially obscuring her face. Her garments looked as if they had been made of several different remnants, much like a patchwork quilt that my mother had made for me when I was only four.

As she stood before our table, with all the books and papers cluttering it, she smiled and then looked directly at me. I was taken by her eyes and could do nothing but return her gaze. Of course, to make matters worse, the whole place had stopped in an instant to see what was going on.

"We have seen you in our visions, and you have visited us in our dreams," she began. "And now, we see face-to-face. The moment of greatness is at hand. Civilization's golden age has begun. You and your three friends will rise to great heights, but beware the mighty hand of power. For once in its grasp, you will become mesmerized and see the lie as the truth and the truth as the lie," the old woman recited for all to hear.

When she had finished, before we could say or ask anything, she bowed her head low before us and vanished back into the crowd. No one else seemed to notice how quickly she had gone. Without thinking or uttering a word to the others, I jumped to my feet and ran after the woman. Too many questions were swirling in my mind. I had to know more.

As I ran outside into the crowded street, I looked frantically among the villagers to see any trace of the old woman. Just as I was about to give up, right before I turned to re-enter the bar, I spotted her. In the distance, right where the road made a turn behind a large building, she hobbled slowly on her cane. I wondered how she had covered such a great distance in such a short period of time. But as if to know what I was thinking, she stopped dead in her tracks and turned fully to face me. In an instant, the old woman's visage fell away, and a beautiful young girl had taken her place. She smiled that same curious smile once again and vanished before my eyes.

I was still wondering at the sight when e-Shack came to check on me.

"Are you all right? Where's the old woman?" he asked.

"I didn't catch her," I replied hesitatingly. Since I did not understand what had just happened, I thought it best to keep what I had seen to myself. At least for now.

"Well, let's go! Daylight is a-wasting, and we still have lots to do," e-Shack rattled off as he grabbed my arm and dragged me back inside.

Sitting around the table again, we tried to make some sense out of what had just happened. Several of the local folk in the bar, came around to reassure us. "She's just a crazy old woman that lives on the outskirts of the village. Pay her no mind. She is always coming in here and proclaiming to anyone who will listen how great some total stranger is," explained the barkeep.

"We get a lot of compliments from the travelers, we do," said another villager.

Concerns assuaged, we all pointed our noses back into the inkwells and parchments. All the while, my mind kept replaying the scene over and over. "Have I seen her in my dreams before?" I reflected.

The daylight streaming though the window had announced the arrival of morning well before we were ready to welcome it. The four of us were able to sleep under a real roof that night, thanks to the kindness of the village mayor himself. We were all very grateful but had precious little time to enjoy this interlude—Menou had come banging on the front door quite early.

"Fifteen minutes and we will have to be on our way," Menou shouted. So we choked down a quick breakfast, thanked our hosts once again, and set off to find our horses within the caravan that was forming along the main street.

We didn't seem to be the only ones blurry eyed; some of the guards looked worse than they did when they had dressed as women. With one mighty "FORWARD" from Arioch, we were off. As the village faded in the distance, I was reminded once again of the old woman's words—an exaltation and a warning.

The way seemed easier now that we had crossed the river. I was told that this road was nothing compared to the great processional road of the plains. Once we reached the outer cities, it would take us the rest of the way to Babylon. With each passing day, the roads became more defined, uncharacteristic of the desert terrain that we had been used to. Villages became towns, and the towns became great walled cities.

We did not mingle with the local cultures. We always camped on the edge of a settlement while others went inside and negotiated for needed supplies. It was safer that way, they routinely explained, but my mind was always wondering what kind of lives the people lived in these places. They probably wondered the same things about us.

One night, Menou explained to us that an ornately decorated wall surrounded the main city of Babylon. And that twelve distinct city-states made up this wall.

"These cities are all a part of the great wall that protects the kingdom of Babylonia. Each city is within sight of Babylon at the center," he explained. "Four major cities mark the northern, southern, eastern, and western poles. There are a total of eight minor cites, two between each of the major cities, that form the rest of the connecting walls. These areas together make up the great outer wall, and thus, connect all twelve of the cities together. The major cities are then connected via road and waterway to one of the four main gates of Babylon. This allows for ease of commerce between all areas and for all farmland to be totally contained within the outer circle. A complex system of water canals provides irrigation, transportation, and domestic supplies of fresh water—compliments of the Euphrates River. You'll learn all about it when we get there."

Hanan could barely contain himself he had so many questions, but Menou was finished.

"No more questions," Menou insisted. "You need your rest. Besides, you will all see it tomorrow."

Our long journey was about to come to an end. That night in the tent, we lay there silently contemplating, about the city, about our classes, about our future in this strange land. Home never seemed so far away, and yet, I could strangely hear my father's voice whispering comfort in my ear.

The next morning in camp, there was a renewed sense of purpose. Home, at least for our captors, was just around the corner, and they could almost smell it. With the provisions packed and breakfast a fading memory, we were on our way.

I must admit even my heart was beating excitedly. I found myself wanting to go faster and faster. What was taking so long? I thought. We appeared to be moving in slow motion. And when I had reached the point where I just couldn't take it anymore, we were there.

And what a "there" it was. Even from a great distance, the walls gleamed and the towers loomed large. Rising from the sparseness around it, a great, continuous wall rose straight up into the air. Light shimmered across its surface as we pressed onward, drawing ever closer.

It took us another three hours before we finally arrived at the western gate. A huge stone visage stared menacingly down at us. The face was that of a warrior with a grand headdress, piercing eyes, and a sword. A large rectangular shield that connected to the ground covered the body. The great walls too were covered with other such warrior displays.

Arioch left the caravan to approach the great gate. A pool of water separated the road from the bottom of the gate. Arioch positioned himself squarely before the shield of the warrior, and after a few hand signals, the stone warrior began to lower his shield and bridge the water.

As the shield came down, so also did our jaws. The sight that we beheld was so far beyond anything that could have been described to us with mere words. First of all, it was green. The processional road extended along vast tracts of land, which were covered with trees. And at the end of the road, a terraced palace, like a jewel in a king's crown, beckoned the viewer to come closer. An enchantment had seized my heart.

Once inside, the full majesty of the city, or should I say cities, came more clearly into view. Behind us stood the great wall city of the western gate. There were grand balconies and walkways that hung in midair. There was also a forty-foot-wide waterway, which seemed to encircle the interior side of the walled cities. It stretched as far as I could see in both directions. In addition to the grand waterway, there were two smaller waterways flanking both sides of the processional road. The many colors of vegetation that thrived in this place were brilliantly reflected on the calm surface of the dark waters.

With the exterior gate now clanging back into its closed position, another road surface rose from beneath the forty-foot waterway to allow us to continue our journey toward the central city, Babylon itself. As we crossed, the cool waters washed away some of the dirt from the wheels of the many carts and delighted the hooves of the tired horses.

We had almost reached our final destination, and even the horses knew it. I felt that I would be saying a difficult "goodbye" to an old friend when I dismounted for the final time. My father had always taught me to be grateful to those who helped me in life, and that that included the beasts of the field. And now that we had reached our final destination, I did just that. One last treat, one last pat on the nose, and the horses were led off to the stables.

I think that Abed was the most relieved at this point. He had never fully grasped the joy that riding could be. And here we stood, with the rest of the captives, waiting to see where they would put us. We had not waited long before Menou directed us into a side chamber. Here he introduced us to Melzar.

"During your studies at Babylon, Melzar will be your direct report," Menou announced. "It is he that will make arrangements for your sustenance, housing, and daily schedule. Think of him as your 'den mother,' and don't give him any cause for grief. You will regret it, I can assure you." He then turned to Melzar, "They're all yours." No more to say, Menou took his leave of us.

Melzar took charge, "You are about to enter the main, center city. We call it Babylon. This city houses the palaces of the king and those who serve in his court. Babylon is devoted to the understanding of science, astrology, and the mystic arts. It is here that you will begin your three-year training in the Chaldean ways of life. Only those of you who demonstrate the highest mastery of these sciences will stand before the king."

"Who will make the determination of who is best?" Hanan had blurted out, startling half the group.

"That determination will be made by the king himself," Melzar answered gruffly. "Now, if you will follow me, I will escort you to your quarters."

We sat off around some large hanging balconies laden with lush vines and flowers and came upon a magnificent gate. This gate was covered with hundreds of carvings of lions, dragons, and bulls—a most foreboding site to anyone wishing to enter without invitation. As we approached, an opening appeared in the mouth of one of the dragon's heads near the ground. We stepped through in single file.

If anyone in our group had remained unimpressed to this point, they could deny it no longer. Gold adorned this city like grains of sand cling to the beach.

"What do they do, make the stuff here?" Hanan commented upon seeing so much gold.

"When do we eat?" Abed asked, as if to disregard any substance that could not be consumed. e-Shack and I gazed around in amazement at ornately decorated fountains, the colorful tile work that adorned the buildings, and the exuberant faces of the inhabitants. Two people around us were engaged in a heated discussion about something related to "energizing forces." I couldn't make out most of it; my Chaldean still was not up to par.

It was at just this moment something happened that would cast suspicion upon our individual safety throughout our time in Babylon. As we walked beneath the edge of one of the terraced gardens, a large pot, filled with dirt and plants, came crashing down and shattered at our feet, narrowly missing my head. We were all shaken, and the incident was chalked up to a careless gardener, but I wasn't so sure. I had the feeling that we were being watched, even stalked, and that we would all have to be on our guard from now on.

"No time for sightseeing," Melzar announced, shaking off the incident. "You will all be given a full tour of the city tomorrow. But for now, follow me to the kitchens before I show you to your quarters."

We ambled distractedly forward, consumed by the sheer size of it all. Interconnecting arches seemed to grow out of the ground and intersect hundreds of feet in the air. Buildings stacked upon buildings defied gravity itself. Before we could marvel at anything more, we crossed a narrow bridge that led us up to a wide pillared porch with outside seating.

"Please seat yourselves, and I will let the cooks know that you have arrived," Melzar's voice trailed off as he entered the front doorway.

We all sat and talked about the great things that we had already seen and wondered aloud about all the mysteries that Babylon might hold. As we sat, eagerly awaiting our dinner, Abed began to speak about his favorite foods and how he hoped that they might be able to read his mind and serve just what he had imagined. e-Shack and I were still commiserating about that unfortunate pot incident, but before we could discuss it in depth, the trays of food began to arrive.

All manner of fresh fruit were brought out first, followed closely by the most delicious breads that I have ever tasted. Next came the meat accompanied by soups of every form. Something about the meat, however, made me cautious about eating it, so I chose the soups instead.

Upon completing the main courses, we were then treated to a dessert tray of the finest confections, very tasty, and from the look on Abed's face, quite satisfying.

Stuffed but content, we were escorted away to our quarters. Our dormitories were two-storied buildings that were all interconnected. Each had a rooftop garden, two bedrooms upstairs, and a large study area downstairs. And since the buildings were built on a slight hillside, there was a terraced effect to the rooftop gardens. Each had a splendid view of the campus courtyard. This would be our home for the next few years.

Abed, Hanan, e-Shack, and I took a three-roomed dormitory together and settled in for the evening. It was hard to believe that just last night, we had been sleeping in tents in the desert. With all this luxury around us, I knew that we would have to be careful not to forget where we came from.

The next morning, a distant "bong" of a bell broke the morning silence. It wasn't at all unpleasant, but warm and inviting to the new day. We all arose and dressed in long emerald green robes which had been laid out for us while we slept. All first-year students wore similar clothes. Once dressed, we assembled in the dining area (the same in which we had taken our first meal) to begin breakfast.

Melzar appeared from behind a large flowering bush just as we were about to finish up. It was at this moment that we first began to understand the daunting tasks that were to be set before us. Melzar began his first-day-of-term greeting as follows:

"You have all been brought here by the express command of the king of Babylon himself. Each of you has been tested and found to possess some special gift that we will endeavor to refine and develop during these next three years. This is not an easy path you are about to embark upon. You will be required to focus your mind and your passions upon one solitary goal. There will be no time for adolescent bickering or infighting during your time here. You will all be kept together. Your contact with others who have been brought here like yourselves will be strictly controlled. You have free roam of the courtyard areas and the classroom buildings. Any other locations within Babylon are forbidden during your first year, except during special circumstances.

"Now that we have set a few ground rules," Melzar continued, "we can get down to business. These are your instructors." And six ancient-looking men dressed all in gold appeared before us. "Six students each will be paired with one teacher for the entire year."

Melzar took the first six students that he saw and began to pair them up with one of the six teachers. As we saw the divisions of six coming down to us, we made sure that we four would be in the same grouping of six. And sure enough, we, together, were presented to the last of the six teachers.

We seemed to have run out of luck though. This man was the smallest and frailest one of them all. He would have been more suited to teach basket weaving than young energetic men. But be that as it may, we were finally started.

CHAPTER 2

Blind Sight

The small man in the golden robes stood before us (not one of us in our youth was shorter than him), looked up into our eyes, and began to speak. Try as I might, I could not understand a single word. I glanced quickly at Hanan, thinking this to be some language that he might have been taught, but his face registered the same confused gaze that I surely must have expressed myself. As we mumbled amongst ourselves trying to figure out how to communicate with this strange man, he smiled, laughed a suspicious laugh, and motioned us to follow him.

"You have much to learn," he finally began. "So let us begin with language. It is one foundation upon which understanding can begin. You will learn, however, that it has its limitations.

"I have been told that Hanan has been instructing you in some of the basics of the Chaldean tongue," the small man continued. "We shall enlist his special skills to instruct you all. You will grow to understand that everyone you meet knows something that you do not, and thereby, can be a teacher to you. No matter what their station in life, the lesson that they teach you, if missed, could mean your destruction."

"Excuse me, but by what name should we call you?" Hanan asked.

"I am known by many names, and its sound is different upon the wind than it is under the water. But for now, you may call me Sol, for I will be your guide through the darkness," Sol answered. "Our first lesson begins with darkness. I want you to close your eyes. What do you see?"

"Nothing," Abed blurted out. "How can we see without eyes?"

"Ah," Sol continued. "That is the question, isn't it? How to see without using our eyes. There are different ways, however, to see without eyes. One of them is to rely more heavily upon the other physical senses. What do you hear? What do you smell? What do you feel upon your skin? All these senses can give you information about where you are and what is around you. This is where we will start. Later you will learn about senses that are not physical and how they can give you information that may contradict what your physical senses tell you.

"You may open your eyes and take a seat on the benches behind you," said Sol, pointing toward a set of benches that I could have sworn was not there when we had arrived. "Your first level of understanding is to be constantly aware of the dynamic world around you. Your mind only wants to concentrate on what it sees for a short amount of time. So it takes a static image of what you have seen and remembers it thusly until it re-engages the object. The problem is that while the mind is distracted with other things, the reality that the static image represents changes. Only when the eyes re-engage the scene does the mental image become updated. But if you bring to bare your complete store of senses, your mental image can be consistent with the dynamic world."

"Wow," e-Shack gasped. "Now that's deep."

"Your homework for tonight is to sit in the courtyard, close your eyes, and visualize what is happening around you using your other senses. Form a picture in your mind of what you think is before you. Open your eyes and evaluate how closely your mental picture matches what your eyes see. You will find that you get better with practice, so practice, practice, practice." And with that admonition, Sol gave us over to Hanan for our language lessons.

As the weeks progressed, so did our interest in the wonders that we were awakening to. Our physical eyes had indeed limited our sight. They showed us what we wanted and expected to see, things that would make sense to our logical minds. I soon learned, however, that I could sense the presence of another even before they stepped into view. And that things that didn't make sense didn't need to anymore.

I found myself being more aware of Hanan's thirst for learning, Abed's enjoyment of the tactile world, and e-Shack's rising to a higher plane. We were all changing, growing in ways that we had not known were even possible. We even began to see the earth differently—not as something to use, but as a partner on our voyage through this realm.

But, be that as it may, we were still young men. And as young men, we found ways to stir up some trouble from time to time. About two months into our training, the heavy workload and unending homework finally got the better of us. We decided to sneak out of the confines of our little world and see more of the famous city of Babylon. As we edged our way along the outermost buildings, we saw a great pool of water with lush vegetation all around it. What impressed us most, however, was that at one end stood a fifty-foot-tall statue of a woman kneeling and pouring water from a hug jug. It was as if the river Euphrates itself was being poured into the pool.

We found it relatively easy to slip unseen through the heavy underbrush and get closer to the great statue. There were strange sparkling lights coming from the area where the water splashed into the pool. We wanted to get a closer look. It was amazing, like looking into the twinkling night sky. I remember we all stood mesmerized until a passerby broke our concentration.

"Let's get back to the dorm before we're missed," e-Shack whispered. And we followed him back to the safety of our rooms.

The next morning we were all startled to life by a heavy scratching on the wall outside. No one could muster the courage to go out and see what it was, so we all scurried to the window—clustered tightly together. As I arrived first in the ensuing rush, I was bumped, rather unceremoniously, through the open window. After landing in the bushes beneath, I was immediately attacked by a huge fur ball. More tongue than fur, I realized that the cause of all this uproar was nothing more than a field worker's lost dog. How he had gotten into the palace grounds, I did not know. But here he was, and he didn't look as if he were about to go away anytime soon.

We were stuck with him, it seemed. And so we brought him in and proceeded to clean him up and give him some food and water. Contented, he lay down in the corner. And just in time too, we were late for morning lessons, so off we ran.

Today we were going to get to see a bit more of the kingdom, for we were going outside the palace walls to begin lessons on plant compounds and their many uses. It was a beautiful day, as almost all days had been since we had arrived. A gentle breeze blew through a couple of huge, old trees by the western gate by which we left the palace grounds. The land seemed to roll and twist into unseen reaches.

Many fragrant smells tantalized our senses. Sol led us to a quiet area of arbors and stone tables covered with many jars of various colors.

"Today," Sol expounded, "you begin your training on the many applications of plant compounds—how we find them, the part of the plant that is used, how the compound is prepared, and dosages." As the others gathered around, something caught my eye off in the trees. I had the sneaking suspicion that we were being watched.

Perhaps, I thought, I could draw them out if I pretended to be so engrossed in the lesson (as everyone else seemed to be) that whomever it was, felt comfortable enough to get closer. We had been in lessons for at least two hours, and I must admit that I found the lesson so interesting that my concentration on the intruder lapsed from time to time.

Just when I had about given up on them tipping their hand, I saw some movement in the underbrush a short distance behind where the class was eagerly testing a melancholy remedy. I seized the opportunity to circle around behind the intruder and confront them directly. What met my eyes was something of a mystery. I confronted not an intruder, but a messenger who all the time had been luring me into a meeting, a secret meeting. He was ancient of visage but with youthful eyes. His robes were vibrant red trimmed in gold. He spoke not a word, but took an object from his robes and placed it upon the ground. It shimmered like gold but was transparent like glass.

He nodded once, took two steps backward into the underbrush, and vanished. But how could someone wearing such a radiant robe vanish into the green wood? I questioned. As I stood amazed, a twinkle of light met my eye from the ground where the mysterious stranger had left the object taken from his robes. It too seemed to appear and then disappear into the grass on which it lay.

I suddenly realized that I had been gone too long. I could hear e-Shack calling for me. Quickly, I snatched up the coinlike object from the ground and headed back to the class site.

"I'm over here," I yelled.

"Daniel, you can't go wandering off like that. We were worried, plus you are missing valuable class time," e-Shack reprimanded.

As I tried to explain, my gaze crossed that of Sol's. There was a "knowing" in his eyes that I could not understand. With a twinge of a smile, he beckoned us all back to our studies.

That night, e-Shack, Hanan, and Abed were all trying to explain the parts of the class that I had missed.

"You see," began Hanan, "if you have been bitten by a poisonous tree serpent, you can mix these two plant leaves together with this root, boil for one hour, then swallow just one sip, and it will counteract the poison in your system."

"Oh, oh," interrupted Abed, "this is my favorite. In order to avoid being sickened by these bulbous mushrooms"—they look very much like the edible kind—"you simple take a small amount of the stem, crush it in the pestle, dry it in the sun for two days' time, grind it to a powder, then place a pinch of it on your tongue every day for a week. You will run a little fever, but it will make you immune to this mushroom's toxins."

The palace was always so beautiful at night. The lamps were lit and the many fountains reflected their glow. It was at that moment that I remembered the coin that the stranger had left for me. I had not had time before to even examine it closely, let alone consider why it had been given to me.

As the others were still discussing the day's lessons, I was able to steal away to an area where the light would be better and I would not have to try to explain what I obviously didn't know how to explain. From the moment that I pulled the coin from my robes, it glittered more brightly than gold. It had markings of some kind of language written along the outside edge. In the middle of one side was a single symbol that looked sort of like an M. On the other side was the symbol of a bird with outstretched wings.

I decided to lay the coin on my palm to get a better look, and that's when it happened.

The coin immediately began to float just above my hand, and then it began to spin. As I watched it, the light that it reflected began to change. It began to point—northwest, I think. As I was checking the stars to verify the direction, I instinctively sensed someone approaching. In an instant, I returned the coin to my robes.

"How are you this evening?" I heard a man's voice entreat.

"Fine," I responded. "Is that you, Menou?"

"Yes. Sorry that I haven't been around as you were getting settled. Are things going well?" Menou continued.

"Yes, yes, they are going quite well. Our studies have been intense so far, but very exciting," I commented.

"Good to hear that. Ashpenez has been asking after your welfare. I shall let him know that you and your friends are well. He expects to be back in the city in a few more days. I am sure that he will stop by and see you for himself." Menou broke off his conversation and turned to head back to the king's quarters. "I must get back. Have a good evening, Daniel."

"Thank you," I responded and then decided to head back to the dormitories myself. I was starting to realize that I would need Hanan's help in deciphering the writing on the coin. Perhaps if we both put our heads together, we could come to some sort of conclusion that made sense.

We took rubbings from the coin, both sides, and the edges, so that we had something that we could look at without arousing as much attention as pulling out the glistening coin might get. The sun was going down, but we still had time to get to the main library and at least start a search for answers.

Hanan and I slipped through the crowd milling about the library entrance and found ourselves buried behind thousands of scrolls in a remote corner.

"We're looking for something to do with Ma-ji," remarked Hanan. "There should be something in this section that will tell us more."

I found a scroll of words and their meanings and searched for the word "Ma-ji."

"Hanan, I've found something . . . look!" I whispered, and we began to read:

> The Ma-ji is a mystic sect known to predate historical accounting. They are believed to be descendants of a group of enlightened souls who possessed magical powers. It is said that they can suspend gravity and walk through walls of solid stone. Their intuitive powers unmask evil and their knowledge of the future allows them to preserve the light for coming generations.

"Is that all it says?" chortled Hanan.

"Well," I responded, "it's a start, isn't it? We have to go!"

And with that, we were back to the dormitory to sleep on this most unusual of problems. But somehow, I knew that what I was looking for was not to be found in any scroll. It was something that I would have to learn as I went along. For good or for bad, I just hoped that I was up to the challenge.

CHAPTER 3

The Midnight Mist

Late one evening, several weeks later, I was awakened in the middle of the night by the screech of a nighthawk. As no one else seemed to be disturbed, I crept as silently as possible from my bed. Dressing quickly, I slipped out onto the moonlit porch. There was not a soul to be found. All the night touches had long since been extinguished; only a rising gray mist visible across the lawn.

It was at that moment that I noticed a dim light moving through the mist. I watched as it came ever closer and strained my eyes to discern the shape of the one carrying the lamp. I could not, however, distinguish the form of the lamp holder due to the brightness of the light as it shot beams in every direction. Suddenly, all movement stopped, and I could just make out a darkened shadow of an arm waving me to come nearer.

I looked around and saw no other but myself. Who could this be? Is it wise to follow a stranger into such a strange mist? I earnestly deliberated with myself.

Before I even had time to make a conscious decision, one way or the other, I found my legs being moved, as if by someone else, in the direction of the mysterious figure. Almost immediately I became engulfed in a mist that was so thick my eyes could not tell left from right. The lamplight that I had been drawn to so intently was now gone, replaced by a soft glow all around me.

I wandered through this strange world and opened all my senses to what might present itself. It was just then that I heard it—faint but oh so familiar . . .

"Mom, Mom, is that you?" I said, barely speaking out loud.

"It has been such a long time since I have been able to see your face and abide in your presence," she spoke, as softly her voice reached my ear. "My journey has been long and perilous, but at last, I stand before you in this place."

"Mom," I cried, "Mom, how did you get here? Where is Dad? And what of my sisters?"

"It's all right. Everyone is fine. But I come to warn you that one you trust will show himself untrustworthy. Follow your heart in this matter and do not let contempt blind you. See with your heart, as you do now through the mist, and let not your eyes deceive."

With that said, her voice faded, and her shadow melted into the night. And before I realized it, I was standing alone amidst the trees. The mist had vanished and so too had my mother.

How I got back to the dormitory, I do not know. But back in the comforts of my room, my eyes overcome with fatigue, I was soon fast asleep. All too quickly, however, morning came and I began to wonder if it all hadn't been just some silly dream.

As we walked to our breakfast meal, I confided to the others the happenings of the last evening. They seemed even more bewildered than I was.

"Maybe it was a dream," mused Hanan. "Perhaps the mince pie didn't sit well with you, or longing for home and family just got the better of your imagination."

"I don't think so," e-Shack responded. "I think that something is going on. Can you remember anything else? Think . . . there has to be some clue that you are overlooking."

"That's all I know," I said, still contemplating each detail. "I have to trust that it will become clearer to me as the event, whatever that may be, comes closer."

Abed was a little too quiet this morning, but we were all rushed off to class before I had had the chance to inquire about it.

Today's lessons were to take us beyond our normal group to a much larger convocation (all students had been called together to be addressed by Arioch himself). We entered a vast stadium with raised seating and found our way down toward the main floor and the speaker's platform.

Students were being brought into the stadium from all directions, each group defined by their robes of distinctive colors and regimental style adornments. In short order, all students were seated and a hush fell over the congregation.

Arioch came from behind a distant pillar and made his way to the center of the stage. I couldn't help but be reminded of that day when I first met him through the smoke and fire in the fields of Thelema. He had a certain way of scaring everyone into silence. I soon noticed that I wasn't the only one sitting unusually straight in my seat.

Arioch began heartily, "I did not want too much of the year to get away before letting each of you know just how proud I am of your commitment to your studies and the progress that you have already made. I know that there are still those of you who harbor ill will against us and do not understand that our intention is for the better good of both your worlds and our own. I trust that each of you, in time, will come to realize that your position here will serve you well personally and be a credit to your homelands.

"Now, to get down to the business at hand, it is customary at this time of the year for there to be a competition held between each of the classes in order to determine which is best. We feel that this encourages camaraderie amongst the groups and develops character.

Part of the excitement of this event is the fact that you have no additional time to prepare. It is very important to always be ready. In battle, your enemy does not allow you the luxury of a cram night before the fray.

"So in the spirit of chaos," he continued, "we have set up a little impromptu challenge. Each group is seated in a special area of the stadium, and if you will be so kind as to check under your seats, there are six different colored scarves placed around. If you find one, untie it and bring it to me."

There was a scrambling about as everyone immediately began bending and craning to see if such a scarf was tied under their seat. One by one, each group's champion moved cautiously toward the front stage.

My group was having a bit of trouble finding anything remotely looking like a scarf under our seats . . . some chicken bones and a few scraps of a wooden sign, but no scarf. Finally, e-Shack, sitting on the end of a row and looking around under seats with no occupants, found a black scarf. He was the last one of the six groups that moved toward the stage area.

"Now the rules are as follows: A panel made up of your six instructors will ask questions in turn of the six champions. They cannot, of course, ask a question of their own pupils. I will decide if a question is unreasonable, and each student will have the same amount of time to answer. A student may propose an answer on his or her own but will also be allowed to choose one from his or her own class to assist. Members of a class cannot collaborate or assist in any way the champion or the chosen advisor. The group with the most correct answers wins the tournament and a free pass for the entire group to the southern city of Pandora for the day. Questions? If we are ready then, let's begin."

A hush fell upon the crowd as the instructors were seated on the stage in front of the champions. The instructors were seated upon a high platform facing the crowd. The first instructor began the questioning.

"What are the three main ingredients in a fainting medicine?"

A boy, holding a blue scarf, looked thoughtfully off into the air, thinking.

"You have thirty seconds," Arioch called out. "Do you wish to choose an advisor?"

"No, I know this one," he said as a look of happy realization just swept over his face. "Garlic, rosemary, and sage. That's my answer."

"Very good."

And the next instructor began. On and on they went, most champions being able to answer without a need to call on an advisor. This seemed to be just a warm-up round. As each round progressed, however, the questions became increasingly complex. To this point, all the groups were equal in points; but now, answers rightly and fully given merited additional points, and the point gaps began to widen.

Being one of the smartest in our group, e-Shack easily kept us at the highest point level. Only one other group was ahead of us, the purple team, and they had us by only one point.

"This is the last round," Arioch stated, as the tension in the crowd reached an almost unbearable level. "The one with the most points at the end will be winner."

The blue team and the red team were too far behind to make up the needed points in just one last question. It would be between yellow, green, purple, and black. Being the black scarf team leader, e-Shack still trailed the purple team, but neither the yellow nor the green teams could be ruled out at this point.

As these last questions came, no champion would dare try to answer without consulting the best in his or her class on the topic at hand. But question after question met with failed response after failed response. It was down to the purple team and the black team.

The next instructor looked intently upon the purple team's champion. "Your question," he began, "requires only one word as the answer."

A great silence filled the stadium as all seemed to hold their collective breath.

"What is lived in a moment, takes a lifetime to experience, and belies your conscious thought?"

A look of utter confusion filled the girl's face holding the purple scarf. And from where I sat, the reaction was none too different from her classmates seated just behind her. She turned slowly, as if lost in thought, and gazed into the eyes of her team, trying to find a face with any sign of recognition of the answer. But there was no knowing in those eyes that she met. What would she say? "One word is the answer," was all she kept saying.

"Time is up. What is your answer?" Arioch had reported far more quickly than seemed possible.

"I do not know," she said sadly, her head bowed to the floor in front of her.

"Very well, then," Arioch continued. "You have the same question posed to you, e-Shack. And since you have already heard the question, your time to respond will be cut in half. Do you wish to choose an advisor?"

"Yes," e-Shack announced immediately.

"Who?" Arioch responded.

This time, e-Shack's answer was not nearly as quick. He looked from Hanan to me and back to Hanan again. Hanan could answer any question on history, science, or language, but riddles were not his best area. I then began to notice that his eye had begun to settle upon me, and I had no clue at all.

Please choose Hanan, I thought, not me—I don't know! But in total disregard for the look of horror on my face, e-Shack blurted out, "Daniel."

"You together have only fifteen seconds," Arioch hurriedly interjected. "Go!"

I ran to the stage and asked why he had chosen me, because I hadn't a clue. All e-Shack said was, "You know, Daniel, you know! Don't use your logic, use your instinct and answer whatever comes to mind when they ask you."

It felt like to me that time stopped after that. The whole world moved in a kind of slow motion. What was the question again, my mind was asking, and as if to respond to its own question, the words began to recite themselves inside my head:

> What is lived in a moment?
> Takes a lifetime to experience?
> And belies your conscious thought?

My eyes looked through a haze of cloud and nothingness. No answer, no word, no champion's circle . . .

"Don't think," e-Shack kept whispering into my ears, which were barely working. "Don't think the answer, know the answer."

"Time's up," yelled Arioch. "What is your answer?" e-Shack's voice was silent, as he looked straight into my eyes. "Well—"

"Dreams," I whispered, more to the ground than to anybody else.

"What," the instructor inquired. "What was that again?"

"Dreams!" I shouted for all to hear. "Dreams are lived in a moment, can take a lifetime to experience, and belie conscious thought—Dreams."

"Your answer," the instructor began (while the whole crowd waited as if seated on the edge of a sword), "is correct!"

All the groups came together as one in a tremendous cry of both relief and jubilation. But we had not won; we rather had tied with the purple team. Arioch must have felt that we had gotten what he wanted for us out of this exercise and decided to let both groups go to Pandora for the day.

Pandora sits in the southern part of the kingdom. It is renowned for its carnival atmosphere. We entered the city to the sound of minstrels and street performers. Everywhere there were brightly colored costumes and feats of the most unusual for strength and agility. A man was even attempting to walk a rope—with nothing but his arms for balance—high above the streets.

This was a city of amusement, and many there were that came and went through its cobbled streets, seeking pleasant diversion from life's toils. Laughter rang out from the ramparts and even the elders became as children. I too was soon swept away by the merriment. It had been a very long time since I had last forgotten about schoolwork and studies.

The day passed quickly, as most such days do, and found us all tired yet delighted as we watched the lights fade upon the waters behind the ferry that slowly carried us back to the palace grounds and home.

CHAPTER 4

The Lion and the Labyrinth

We had now been at Babylon long enough to pretty much have free roam of the palace grounds, and upon occasion, the outer cities were available to us. I became a regular at the horse stables once I learned that we were permitted to ride whenever we could find a free moment or two.

In reuniting with my horse of the exile, I had come up with a better name than Horsy. I named him Wildfire after the day that I was taken from the fire and thick smoke of my homeland invasion. Whenever I had any time at all, I would run through the hidden dragon's mouth gate of the palace grounds and light upon the stables. The stable hands had grown quite accustomed to seeing me at such odd times and had made it a point to let only me ride Wildfire.

He would become wild-eyed upon my arrival—furiously pawing at the ground. For, you see, I would only need the bridle, which hung ready for use by Wildfire's stall. No time for the saddle, or even a blanket. We would be off in a flash of white into the empty pastures surrounding the horse stables.

Sometimes, we would ride for fifteen minutes, if that was all the time we had. But usually we would be out for at least an hour or two, and on occasion, well into the night. We had our own secret spot by a small stream with towering trees whose branches swept the ground with every light breeze. Many a sunset I did sit and ponder upon life there. Wildfire was just happy to be out in the sweet-smelling (and tasting) fields.

On one such night, after the sun had set and I had retaken horseback to return to the palace, I met a most unwelcome troop blocking my path. They were dressed all in black and hooded so that I could not know who they were. Only one spoke and directed me back through a glen to a small group of buildings where crops were stored. Hidden away, I had not noticed it on any of my previous visits to this part of the kingdom. There was an eerie silence about this place. Where were the workmen? Where were any people at all?

I was directed inside the gates and led up a staircase to a balcony overlooking the main road entering the village. The other horsemen waited outside the gates, and I could just hear the furious groans of a wild beast. As we both gazed silently upon the entrance, an awful sight met my eyes. Four men carried a cage suspended upon two poles. A single lion, such as I had never seen for its size, struggled and fought against its captivity, causing the men carrying it to nearly fall on several occasions.

Finally—exhausted—the men dropped the cage, but more violently then they had planned, for it bust open upon striking the ground. A melee ensued as men scrambled both inside and outside the gates. Two of those carrying the loathsome beast made it through the gates before they were slammed shut against the fury raging within. The other two men were left trapped between the lion and no escape. It happened in only a moment.

As their lifeless bodies lay mangled and bleeding, the hooded figure spoke to me of the village maze. "There is only one way out—save the gate by which you just entered. It is there, in the far back corner, a staircase to freedom, a staircase to life if you reach it before the lion gets you."

With no more to reveal, he flung a rope up over a great beam at the top of the gate and swung to safety. The rumble of horse hooves riding swiftly away left me and a very angry beast alone in the maze. A seething hatred filled his eyes . . . and at that moment, I was the only one around upon whom to vent it.

Suddenly, in one bound of its powerful flesh, the great lion jumped onto the balcony where I now stood. I turned to a ladder that was laid upon the side of the two-storied building and raced to the top just before it was ripped out from underneath me.

From there, I could see the many levels of housing and the thatched roofs of this simple community. It seemed that it was only for use during the harvest, when workers would need to tend the crops for several weeks at a time. Some roofs were high and some were low, only one story. I could see many ladders that aided in entry to the higher rooms but which would not provide the lion access. But to the lion's favor, any roof could be accessed via another roof, if accessed properly. And as I watched the lion still clawing at the wall beneath me, I could see that he too was beginning to realize there were other ways to achieve his goal.

Quickly, he leapt from the balcony and raced between the mud-bricked buildings. He was gone, but I knew that my life depended upon me reaching the back stairway before he did. I would not have time, just like those two men, to even think about getting out of the way if he caught up with me again.

A maze is best solved from a high vantage point. But even after you plan your way through, the maze has a way of tripping you up once you get down into its belly. I could see a way out, but to my dread, it involved one area where

I would have to cross between two buildings in plain view of intersecting streets.

I would have to risk it. Maybe I could create a diversion for the lion. Maybe the lion had already found its way out and was gone into the night. Maybe the lion was going to devour me no matter what I did.

I have never been one to wait for trouble to come to me. I would rather meet it on my terms, even if my terms have no advantage. With one mighty heave, I thrust my body forward onto a nearby roof, nearly toppling off the other side before stabilizing myself. I stopped, heart racing, listening . . . nothing . . . not one sound.

From rooftop to rooftop, up one ladder and down another, I made my way toward the prize. Now I stood at the intersection that had so troubled me when I could look down upon the maze . . . still no other noise was heard. I, however, must have sounded like an elephant trying to sneak past a guard while treading upon a thousand peanut shells.

Looking carefully, I noticed a large pile of wood and debris stacked against the building next to me. A ladder on the opposite wall was the only thing that stood between me and freedom, life and death. Surely the lion was not in this place, but dark corners could hide anything.

Not knowing what else I could do, I ran with all my might—I ran toward the ladder. But somewhere just before I reached it, a massive force struck me from my left and threw me into the pile of debris stacked against the village hut. With one mighty crash, the wood tumbled to the ground, knocking me face down into the dirt.

A terrible whimper was all I heard from beneath the rubble. It had destroyed the flimsy ladder but had created a makeshift stepping bridge up to the village wall and the back staircase. All I had to do was to climb the woodpile to safety, but as I began to climb, I noticed the lion trapped beneath a large timber. His eyes seemed different now. The pain he was in had somehow destroyed the anger within him. His somber eyes pleaded for help. His furious roar had become a painful howl.

I was halfway up to the top and freedom when I realized that I could not leave him there. I don't know why; he was trapped—I was safe. If I tried to help him, he could still rip me apart in one swipe of his mighty paw. As crazy as it sounds, I went back. I went back to see if I could help . . . to see if I could free him.

The beam was heavy upon him, and he was bleeding. I searched for a fulcrum that I could use to leverage the large and heavy wood. Finally, I was able to free up a large enough piece of wood that might work, and with a heave, I put all my weight onto it. The beam didn't move. It wasn't enough; I had to find something longer. The lion would surely die if I could not free him soon.

Unable to find anything else, I pulled this board from the heap and tried it in a different location. This time, the massive beam that held the lion pinned to the ground moved. It moved just enough to release its hold on the lion. But I would have to stay and continue steadfast until the lion was completely escaped, leaving me at his mercy. Undaunted, I pushed hard while talking to the lion, encouraging him to crawl and slide from under the beam. Somehow he understood.

He moved slowly, and I was almost at collapse, before he was finally clear of the beam. It hit the ground with a deep thud, and I fell to my knees overcome with fatigue, looking into the now puzzled eyes of the lion. He regained his strength in an instant and stood before me as huge as ever.

I had made the wrong decision, I thought. This is it; I am done for. And just before I fell full to the ground, the lion leapt straight at me—but jumping over me, he made his way up the debris to the top of the wall. He stopped only once more to reconsider me, before vanishing down the back staircase and into the forest.

I couldn't believe it. Just when I thought that things had once again come to a final end, I was saved. And as I lay there wondered about all this, I could here the snorting and stamping of a familiar friend just outside—Wildfire.

It took me a few moments before I could regain enough strength to clamber my way to the top of the woodpile. Once on top of the back wall, I could see Wildfire's white outline, glowing in the light of the full moon. I don't quite know how I managed it, but the next thing that I remember is arriving back at the stables. I was carried by the stable hands back to my room, and a healer was sent in to attend to my wounds.

"Where have you been?" asked e-Shack, great concern evident in his voice.

"We were so worried when your horse came back without you," chortled in Hanan. e-Shack explained to me how that the stable hands could not calm Wildfire when he arrived back at the stables alone. They tried to put him in his pin, but he broke away and ran back into the darkness.

"That's when they came to get us," e-Shack continued.

"You look a mess, Daniel," Abed added, as if this wasn't evident without saying so. "What happened?"

And I began to explain to them all that had transpired—the hooded men, the village maze, and oh yes, the great big lion. Somewhere in the middle of the telling of this, though, I must have dropped off, for the next thing that I remember is the sun shining through my window and my room empty, save for the healer who had evidently come back to check on my progress.

"Relax, you have been unconscious most of the night and well into the day," the healer remarked softly. "Your wounds have been treated, and there is no sign of an infection. You should be up and about in just a few days, but I don't want you out of that bed without someone here to help you. You are still quite groggy from the medicine that we have given you for the pain.

"That was quite a remarkable feat that you accomplished in the maze," he continued. "Few men would have been able to keep their wits about them long enough to find an escape. And what you did for that lion, that was totally unexpected . . . but shows us how, even in the face of death, you value life above all else."

"But how did you know about the maze and the lion?" I interrupted. "You weren't here when I told the others, and I did not even tell them about going back to rescue the lion."

"You talk in your sleep," he said with a wry bit of wit. "Now drink this and get some more rest."

The liquid took hold rapidly and the world around me began to spin, and my vision blurred. But before I passed out, I questioned through slurred speech, "What do you mean us? You make it sound like there were others . . . like yourself . . . there . . . but no one else . . . alone . . . ."

I was in and out for the next couple of days. When I did finally awaken, I felt brand new. The palace never looked more beautiful, and having my friends fussing over me so much wasn't such a bad thing either.

Once things began to get back to a normal schedule, e-Shack and I returned to the business of finding out just what that coin might mean. Why did it spin in my hand and not his? Why could we find so little information about the words written carefully around the edge of the coin?

Sol had been our teacher for the first year and had become quite a confidant. His only advice was to look inside rather than out for answers of the mind. What was it that he used to say? "The mind is a conduit to the edge of reality"—whatever that meant. But it seemed to us that he was saying not to waste all our time looking for a written answer to our questionings.

From that time forward, we let go of our quest for the why and began looking more for the what. What would this lead us to? As we ambled through the last few days of our first year's classes, we were reminded that a new teacher was about to enter our lives. This thought was quite unsettling to the four of us, as we had grown accustomed to the light in Sol's eyes. He assured us that we would see him again, but I have never been one for goodbyes.

CHAPTER 5

The Second Year

It was still just the group of thirty from Axios that was gathered together—bright and early—on the first morning of the second term. As the new teachers were brought in, there was a determined effort to mix up the classes for the coming year. It was not random, as was the first time; we were now being divided along the lines of our particular "area of promise," as they called it. Some of the groups, I understood easily why they were placed together; the others, I could not make out the connection.

And then the most surprising thing of all happened: The six teachers were placed in a row in front of the prospective students. Each student was taken to the front and placed with a teacher. With all the students placed, save me, I noticed that it was not an even pairing. Some teachers had seven or eight students, and others only three or four. But all teachers were now leaving with their students, leaving me alone to watch them go. e-Shack gave me a quizzical glance as he followed his teacher and two other students from the grounds.

Melzar, the guard placing us in our groups, gave me a quick smile as he waited for the students to leave the convocation area.

"You," he began, "are to be placed in a very special program. You have been observed all year and have been found most promising in the gifts of the dreamtime. You have a propensity to see into the future, to hear its message, and to bridge the divide between now and what is to be."

Okay, I thought, not sure where this was leading to.

"Your teacher will be arriving shortly, and since I have other business," Melzar continued, "I will leave you to his charge. Please wait here patiently for his arrival."

Melzar turned on his heels with a short military turn and walked away into the lush green canopy that surrounded this place.

I waited, and waited, and waited some more. Have they forgotten about me? Should I stay here, or go look for someone to help me. Perhaps my teacher was not able to make it to our meeting this morning. Or perhaps, my teacher was here all along, watching to see what I might do, how I might react to the situation. Sol, of course, had done many such things during his year of teaching us.

I was starting to get a little annoyed. If they were just going to leave me to sit all alone on a bench, then I was going to make some profitable use of my time. I found a piece of parchment and wrote a quick note saying that I could be found in the library, if anyone ever did manage to come along. I left the note under a small stone, and struck out for my second favorite place (the stables being my first, of course).

As I walked along the tree-lined paths toward the library buildings, I was keenly aware of a second presence, unseen and yet as real as the breeze upon my face. I had not been alone; someone was watching and now following me, covert and silent, yet obvious and visible to my nontactile senses.

"Stay hidden, if you like," I whispered, "but I know you are there."

Suddenly, on the very periphery of my vision, I saw a man, small of stature, taking shape before my eyes. It was Sol.

"You have learned well, your first year, but much lies ahead," Sol murmured almost to himself.

We walked along in silence, a slight smile upon my face, happy in knowing that we were going to be together again for another year.

"So where are we going?" I asked at last, understanding that I would not, as usual, get a straight answer.

"We are off to see a man about a horse," he said with a hint of mystery to his voice.

Nope, I thought, I'm not biting. And I restrained myself from asking the logical question. We'll just see what this first lesson turns out to be when we get there.

It wasn't long before we came to a familiar spot—the horse stables. I gravitated immediately toward the stall where Wildfire was kept, but he was not there. "Out in the pasture, I suppose," I commented to Sol.

"He is there," Sol said, pointing to the far-end doors. A stable hand was just bringing him in. He was groomed and already fitted with his bridle.

"Are we going for a ride?" I entreated.

"There is a journey we must take—alone and together we will find our common paths." Sol had answered my question with a riddle, but I was ready for anything. Or at least I had thought so at the time. "Ride toward the great forest and find there your path twenty yards south of the boat rock. It is well hidden from the untrained eye. Do not miss it. I will meet you halfway down the path." Sol's instructions were precise and yet ambiguous. How was I to know when I was halfway down the path?

Before I could rattle on any further, a slap on the rear of Wildfire saw me exit out of the stables like something shot out of a catapult. Wildfire always understood even the slightest turn of my knee or even the very object that my eye was engaged upon and he would run in that direction.

It was a beautiful sunny day with a light, warm breeze blowing through the high grasses that we now sailed upon.

We sailed upon this grassy sea until we reached the edge of the great forest. Trees grew thick and tall here, timeless in their austere grandeur and mystifying in their windswept silence. We slowed to a gentle walk as I attempted to locate anything that might resemble a "boat rock." With the presence of one at once hidden and yet in full view, the boat rock came unexpectedly to light.

How could I not have noticed it before? How many times had my eyes scanned and re-scanned this very spot. Only when I looked within could I see the life all around me, each a signpost guiding me to the path. A path of undetermined length and one too narrow for Wildfire. I must go alone.

Once dismounted, I entreated Wildfire to wait for me while I searched the beyond. No sooner had I entered these hallowed grounds than I became infused with a great sense of harmony, of oneness. You know that feeling when the hair tingles on the back of your neck . . . that is how much this place grabbed me. I tried to focus on the destination that I was to seek but kept getting lost in the life all around me. Sounds echoed through the wood reminiscent of a distant past. Unseen animals sidled nearby un-ensnared by my presence. It was as if I belonged here as much as they did.

Farther and farther I traveled along the faint path, its twists and turns always delighting my senses with new pleasures. It wasn't long, however, before I began to grow worried that maybe somehow I had missed Sol. Had I gone far enough or was I not even close to our rendezvous point? At that moment, as if to preempt any further distress on my part, a clearing appeared, well kept and manicured, standing in stark contrast to the open forest. This area surrounded a great stone statue. I could just make out the features of a man's face. There was an elaborate headdress, somber eyes, and a gaping mouth as if it would swallow the whole world.

I was drawn inexplicably into the mouth, its blackness all-consuming. While my eyes struggled to adjust, I heard a still, small voice. I was not afraid, for I recognized its intonation instantly. Sol.

"You are late, you are very late. What kept you?" he asked derisively.

"Are you sure?" I replied, certain that I could not have been late in my arrival. I had not squandered my time or been drawn from the path, even though many times I was tempted by a noise or sight of great beauty.

"Path. There is no path to this place. What you saw as the path was only your intuition guiding you upon your own path. I, however, have been here for two days' time, waiting," Sol said.

"My sincerest apologies!" I implored. "But where exactly are we?"

"You now stand within one of the twelve masks of life. This mask is known by the name hunger. Other masks are scattered about the realm, hidden to most eyes."

"What is their purpose?" I responded with growing interest.

"There is no purpose, they just are . . . you give them meaning," Sol explained. "What is the purpose of hunger or charity, purity or truth, reputation or honor? They just are!

"Everything is in a state of perpetual being—no yesterday, no tomorrow. In this place, those forces hold true more than in the human world you have come to know.

"Hunger is the first thing that we experience once we leave the womb. It drives us to learning. It carries us through emptiness and want. It allows us to create something better, something grander than those before us.

"All journeys begin here, no matter the path, no matter the perceived destination. This is the womb of life." Thus did Sol begin his instruction.

"Why am I here," I asked tentatively.

"Why are any of us here?" Sol replied with a half smile.

"No, no, no. I don't mean 'why am I here?' in the cosmic sense, but why am I here in the mouth of the mask of hunger?" My question had almost answered itself before I even finished phrasing it. "Oh!" I continued. "I am here precisely because I am hungry—hungry for knowledge, hungry for truth. I seek my place in this world driven by the hunger to know."

Sol simply smiled and nodded slightly. "You are learning to see the obvious. Most people live a lifetime and never even get that far. But seeing that which is hidden—that which lies in shadow and mist—now that takes a little more cunning. Rely upon your intuition and not your logic, and you will know not only your dreams but the dreams that others have dreamed and cannot remember once the morning light appears."

I had been given much to think about that day. As we walked together back to the grassy sea, I could not help but notice a glow about the face of Sol. Maybe it was just the evening sun as it poured out its last vestiges of daylight, but the radiance was nonetheless mesmerizing.

I arrived back at the stables at dusk. Quickly I found my way through the dragon gate and back to my room. Hanan, Abed, and e-Shack were all seated at a large round wooden table that had last year become our study area.

"Where have you been?" came the words from e-Shack. "Melzar came around and told us you were on some sort of overnight training thing. What's been going on? We haven't seen you since we were assigned new teachers."

"I thought that you had just had enough and took off for home," Hanan added.

Not to be left out, Abed threw me a sideways glance and fumed, "You were supposed to be helping me with my research on plant compounds. I am just getting further behind, you know."

"Guys, guys, I am fine. Thanks for asking," I grumbled sarcastically by way of an introduction to my two-day jaunt.

I spent the rest of the night catching them up on all that had transpired. A hush of awe filled the room when I spoke of the twelve masks of life.

"We need to see what we can find in the library on the masks tomorrow, after studies," e-Shack whispered after the others had gone to bed. "Maybe it all has something to do with the coin."

I had not considered this in relation to the coin. As we lay there in the darkness trying to find sleep, I could tell that e-Shack was just as curious as I was about the latest find.

The morning haze gave way to a light blue sky. We each made our way to breakfast and then down to the teachers' cove where we would start the day. Sol was already there, looking quite refreshed, although we had both been up for two days straight.

The classes quickly formed and headed off. Sol and I began a discussion of what held things together as we headed toward the library.

"If you know what binds things together," he explained, "you can better understand what pushes things apart."

I immediately went to the coin in my mind. Could this explain why the coin somehow floated above my hand instead of being attracted to it? I surmised.

"Your assignment for today is to study that subject in the science library," Sol further instructed—leaving me at the front steps of an unfamiliar building. "I will come for you at the end of the day, and we shall discuss your findings."

I entered this library alone. I had been to other libraries but never this one. I did not know that it even existed until now. Sol had obviously been saving it for just the right time.

This library was full of clay tablets instead of scrolls. It was small and confining, with shelves from floor to ceiling and close quarters between each aisle. Only a few other students were to be seen. It was strangely empty.

Rather than focus too much on the environment, I set off to find tablets on the subject of the binding forces of the universe. My first find was a script from ancient Egypt describing the methods used in moving great stones. It explained that one could chose to fight the stones or to work through them to effect their movement. There were drawings demonstrating how it could take up to thirty strong men to move a single cut stone weighing ten tons (even with a well-worn surface to drag it across); but when the proper mind was effected, the stone practically moved itself. Only one man was needed to guide it to the desired location.

This was amazing. Gravity appeared to have been suspended just enough so that the stone no longer rested upon the earth. As I read more about this procedure, I learned that the secrets behind the mind lift had been lost to history—not written down but rather mentored from generation to generation. The clay tablet did go on to say that legend had it that only the Ma-ji were left who know such secrets.

Finally, another source that mentioned the Ma-ji, but what did it mean? The more I read about the Ma-ji, the more I knew that their knowledge—their cunning—was not something that I would learn from reading. Just like a bird is not taught to fly but must learn to fly, I knew that I, too, would have to go through my bumps and bruises before attaining my goal.

In far too little time, the day had faded away, and I was being told that closing time had come. Since none of these tablets could be taken from the library, I would have to suspend my research, at least for now. Reluctantly, I left through the same doors that I had entered early that morning, and who should I find standing just where I had left him? Sol.

"How did you know that I would be coming out at this time?" I asked.

"Oh, just a hunch," Sol answered. "So what have we learned today?"

"We have learned that what appears to be is not always what is. We have learned that the mind has great ability beyond the mundane. We have learned that the hard way isn't necessarily the only way," I recited slowly and deliberately.

"Well done," Sol stated in a pleased manner. And no further questions were asked.

I had never asked Sol directly about the coin. Although I sensed that he knew when it was on my mind. Today had proven that my interest in this subject had been my guide to the tablet. He had facilitated that discovery, and we both knew it. Nothing more needed to be said.

Once back in the dormitory, I lay upon my bed, my head so full of thoughts. The others were still out on the balcony enjoying the evening. Then e-Shack came in to check on me.

"How's it going there, partner?" he commented.

"So many questions, but where do all the answers come from?" I asked.

"Well . . ." e-Shack answered, "books, people, new places—all these things can help you ask the questions. They can even give you their interpretations of what that might mean to you or to anyone else. But when it comes down to the end of the day, the matter is yours to decide, yours to apply, yours to make sense of. I can tell you what I think, but sometimes that just muddies the water."

He didn't even ask me about the day. He didn't have to. He knew all too well the struggle that I was going through without having to name it.

"So what else did you learn about the Ma-ji today?" he continued.

"How did you know that I learned more about them today?" I shot back.

"It is written all over your face, plus I noticed you had the coin in your hand. You haven't done that for quite a while, so I figured that you were probably looking at that again," e-Shack deduced, "also, you talk in your sleep."

I had indeed fallen asleep for a short while once I arrived back in the dormitory. And as I started to wonder what I had been blabbering on about in my sleep, e-Shack spoke up and began to tell me about an old sage that he had met earlier that day. He explained—in hushed tones—that his class had left the palace for a field trip to the western gate city of Varnem. Shortly after their arrival, he had become separated from the class. In running to catch up with his classmates, he had practically run down an old man along a narrow side street.

"I apologized and apologized as I lifted him back to his feet," e-Shack explained. "He was most kind and not the least bit upset at having such a rudeness perpetrated upon him. He smiled a frail smile and insisted that I accompany him to his home, which was not far. What else could I do, even as I watched my class disappear once again into the crowd?

"'Do not worry after your classmates,' the old man told me. 'You will find them again when it is time, and they shall not miss you in your absence.'

"I helped the old man down some steps and into a small but comfortable one-room compartment. He bade me sit while he prepared some refreshment. This place was filled with ancient objects, many that I have only seen in the older scrolls at the library. What kind of life had this man led?

"He sat down with me and we drank. Then my eye was taken by a large tapestry hanging upon the opposite wall. I recognized the symbols of the Ma-ji from the coin that you now hold in your hand. He answered me before I even asked the first question. 'Yes,' he said, 'I once was an active member of the order, many, many years ago now.' And then he spoke of you. I had not told him of you or the coin.

"'Daniel has the gift, and the coin does float in his hand, does it not?'

"'Yes,' I agreed, 'it does, but we do not understand the gift that you speak of.'

"'The gift,' he continued, 'is that of sight beyond sight. A seer of ages will he be that holds the coin suspended in space.'

"'Who is the Ma-ji?' I wondered out loud.

"'They are an ancient order, mystical and wonderful, the keepers of the way upon this earth. They are known and yet unknown. They are seen and yet unseen.'

"'What of the twelve masks of life?' I asked him, sensing that our time was short.

"'These are twelve riddles left upon the earth to guide mankind. One lies deep within the forest, the other upon the plain. Three are together and speak in harmony always, and seven are lost. The Ma-ji have searched far for the remaining seven but have not yet attained their message.'

"Before I could ask the next question, he insisted that I go quickly before I was discovered.

"'Go out the front door and run to the left, take the next two right turns and then a final left. You will find your classmates there,'

"And that was it," e-Shack concluded.

Wow, now that was something to consider. e-Shack hurried back to the balcony so as not to be missed, and I lay there lost in the recounting of all his words. A seer, I am a seer of the ages. What did that mean? What was I to do now? I fell asleep contemplating all these words.

And in my sleep, I dreamed a dreamed. In this dream I visited a country home of friends. There were strange flying creatures outside—like small horses. It was getting late, and I needed to get back, so one of my friends—who was about to leave as well—offered me a ride to the village. We left by horse-drawn cart and entered a large village with multistoried houses lining the road. I got off there and went into a side street between some buildings.

It was then that I saw a door that had been left opened and heard voices coming from deep within. I entered and saw what looked like an archeological dig site. I could see many diggers with strange hats discussing how to proceed in finding something in a large earthen mound.

I somehow wanted to help them—to help them find what they were so driven to uncover. It seemed most important to them. They, however, took no notice of me as I moved among them and came to the edge of the earthen wall. What should I do in order to locate an object buried within this mound? I asked myself. I immediately knew that I was to place my hand facing the wall and move it along slowly. I soon was using both hands—probing the wall—for what I did not know, and I felt no sense of how I was to understand when I had found it.

But find it I did, or should I say, they found me. In one blast of force, a mighty chorus of voices rushed at me and knocked me clean off my feet. I lay flat on my back upon the ground. The diggers were all trying to help me up. What does this mean, and what are you trying to tell me? My mind instantly inquired. The many voices came into a single, clear sound inside my head. They explained that they were sorry to overwhelm me with so much information at once, but there was much to relay and urgency in what needed to be said. It was then that I woke up.

What do they want? What is so important that I must understand? I was so shaken by this strange vision.

I told no one of the dream, not even e-Shack, and it haunted me for months to come.

CHAPTER 6

The Hideaway

S everal days later, while returning from my studies, fate crossed my path once more.

Night had come too quickly for me to arrive back at the dormitory before dark. The lamps were lit, and I had settled in to a leisurely walk along the glistening waterways. A man walked up behind me and whispered that he was Maji and to follow him. By force of habit, I went to respond, but the man just quickened his pace and scurried off. I almost ran to keep up with him.

Finally, we ended at the base of the great statue of a woman that poured out the Euphrates into the palace grounds (I later learned that it was called the Euphrates Maiden). This was the same statue that we discovered upon our first covert visit outside the dormitory area after arriving in Babylon. Before I reached him, he had taken off his robe and slipped silently into the water.

"Hello, hello," I called quietly so as not to attract notice. "Are you there? What am I to do now?"

"Follow me," whispered the voice. "You must swim with me under the great waterfall of the statue. There will be no going back once you have begun, and you will only have enough air to get you safely inside. If you panic, you will drown. Are you afraid? Are you unsure of my motives?"

Logic confounded me. Why should I follow a stranger to what could most certainly be my death.

"Give me one reason why I should trust you," I replied.

"What does your heart tell you?" was his only answer. "We must go now or not at all."

Great, a question answered with a question, but my heart (not my head) had already made the decision, and I found myself removing my outer garments and wading into the waters to follow him to whatever might come.

We swam over to the waterfall and under its pounding edge right up to the foot of the great statue.

"No one can hear us in here," he said in a plain and normal tone. "You must take a very deep breath and follow me under the statue. The waters will carry you rapidly forward. Do not fight it, but rather swim with it. It will carry us both hundreds of feet underground and to the stairs of the hideaway."

"What hideaway . . . hideaway for whom?" But he had gulped his last and disappeared beneath the dark water's surface.

I quickly followed suit and dove beneath the water. I felt myself being sucked right into some large hole just under the surface. He was right—the waters moved very fast. I remembered his advice on not fighting the flow and began to swim with the force that now pulled me into utter darkness.

Too late . . . too late . . . too late . . . I was running out of air, fast, and was unsure of the destination. But just as I thought that I could hold my breath no longer, a strong arm grabbed the back of my undergarments and yanked me clean out of the water.

It was the man who had led me to this dark, damp place. We were on stone steps that rose out of the water and torches were lit along a pathway that ascended up into another chamber. He led the way and I followed silently behind. No words could describe this place and how I felt here. It was very much like the feeling that I had experienced in the forest before discovering the first mask.

I was in awe. The rock face was roughly hewn and glistened with thousands of diamond-like facets. As we rounded the last corner, a room that seemed to be lit by the sun itself caused my eyes to water.

"Wait," I called to the stranger. "I cannot see. My eyes have not yet adjusted to the light."

I heard the footsteps of the stranger pause, and then I felt a hand firmly grasp my arm.

"It is all right. I will lead you forward," the stranger explained. "My name is Moreck. Sorry I did not have a chance to properly introduce myself earlier. I am a member of the sect that you know as Ma-ji. This is the hideaway, or at least one of them, that we use to meet and study the ancient arts."

As my eyes adjusted to the great hallway that came into view, I realized that the roughly sculpted walls were gone. This hallway was as grand as any the palace had to offer. Many ornate doors led off this main passageway, but we continued down its full length, finally arriving at what appeared to be a grand ballroom.

There were groups practicing fencing movements, and others in meditative states. One man, I could have sworn, was actually floating several inches above the marble floor.

Our entrance into this room soon commanded everyone's attention. Moreck led me up to a stage where sat three men, old of age, at a large rectangular table.

"Ah, Daniel," one of the men said as he stood to greet us. "I am Barthalemu. I am the senior member of this sect and welcome you most heartedly to our humble abode. I trust that Moreck has taken good care in getting you here safely and discreetly. I know that you must have a hundred questions, but before we sit down to discuss them, might I suggest some dry garments and refreshment for you both?"

"Thank you, sir," I replied, and Moreck led me into a side chamber. The room was cozy and a fire was blazing in the grate. With fresh garments already laid out for us, we quickly changed and gathered around the hearth. Refreshments were brought in and then it was just Moreck and me once again. "How did you know that I would follow you?" I inquired. "It was a crazy thing to do. It was a crazy thing to ask me to do."

"I am well aware of that," Moreck stated. "I hoped that you had learned enough from Sol to be able to trust your own intuition and not to let logic cloud your actions. And now, here you are. We have been watching you for almost a year."

"It was you," I interrupted. "You are the one that gave me the coin and then vanished into the underbrush."

"Yes, that was indeed me. I was afraid that you would not grasp the importance of the coin or understand its meaning," he continued. "It was more of a test really. The coin's ability to float above the hand of a chosen one has been foretold but never before seen in another. But we did not expect it to spin and change color as it did in your hand."

As we stood there next to the fire and caught up on these strange occurrences, Barthalemu entered the room and requested that we all sit.

"Practical knowledge is a very valuable commodity," he said, coming straight to the point. "The king sends out his warriors all over the world to bring back those items and people that might be able to add to his already great and powerful kingdom. It is he that wishes to rule the entire world from a single throne, a single mind. His scouts too have taken notice of your keen sensibilities and are already working to bring you before him. They would have you in subjection to him, and them. They are strong and trusted advisors to the king and yet they know that you can see right through them. You fill them with fear and foreboding.

"We, however, are not bound to the king's arrogance or pride. Rather, we follow an ancient power that would set up all in equality and harmony. Domination stifles the creative and healing powers of this world. It limits man's vision and destroys hope.

"You must go now," he added. "You will be missed if you are not returned quickly to the place that you are expected. Moreck, I trust you can see Daniel safely home."

"Yes sir! We will leave as soon as Daniel has changed back into the clothes that he was wearing when he arrived," Moreck announced as he stood to whisk me from the room.

"Oh no, not wet clothes . . . and I haven't had a chance to ask a single question," I protested as we walked quickly toward the door.

"Don't worry, your clothes are here, pressed and cleaned," Moreck pointed to garments that had been laid out on the back of a large overstuffed sofa. He waved aside any attempt at further inquiry.

Could these be mine? I thought, but they certainly were, and I changed quickly before we dashed out the door and back into the grand ballroom. It was empty now, but still commanded more than a passing glance as we scurried from the room.

We were traveling down the same long hallway that we had entered, but surely, he could not be planning to get out by the way that we had come in to this place.

We took the same winding staircase back to the watery entrance point.

"We aren't . . ." I grumbled under my breath.

"No, no . . . this way," he pointed to an almost hidden crack in the far-end wall.

We could barely squeeze through the small opening. It was a tunnel just large enough for a small man to stand up in, and barely wide enough for a single-file troop. I could tell that we were heading back to a point close to where we had entered the water.

Just as we arrived at a ladder leading to the surface, I could see that the tunnel continued on and split multiple times. And that wasn't all; I could hear distant noises coming from deep underground, echoing through the many tunnel corridors.

"Diggers," I blurted out. "They sound like diggers, and they are looking for something."

"And how would you know that?" Moreck quickly shot back. He stopped on the ladder just above me and cut through me with a piercing look.

"I had a dream," I answered.

"We don't have time to discuss it now. You will have to let me know about it through Zeke," replied Moreck.

"Zeke! Who is Zeke?"

"The dog. The dog that we sent you last year. He was meant to help us stay in contact with you, but he likes you so much that he rarely leaves your side. When you need him to bring us word, simply tell him to find Madge. He will come to us. Tie your scroll note to his underside. The hair will hide it from prying eyes. We will return messages in the same way. Each message will be encoded. You have the code on the outside rim of that coin that we gave you," Moreck explained as we climbed and climbed up to the surface.

"Code! What code?" I shouted up the ladder.

"Start with the letter that the right wing of the falcon on the front of the coin points to. That corresponds to the first letter of our secret alphabet. Follow on around from the right for each of the other letters. Always translate what you have to say into this format. We'll decipher it and reply."

"And how was I supposed to know all this?" I asked.

"We meant to make contact before now and explain it all, but you have been so closely watched," Moreck rambled distractedly as he poked his head out of the darkened shaft.

We had reached the top and emerged hidden in the undergrowth around the backside of the pool of the

Euphrates Maiden. "Wait here. I will check to ensure that the way is clear. When you see my hand go up, walk onto the path as if you had been strolling there all along." Moreck's voice had become a barely audible whisper once more.

I watched until I could just make out his shadowy form in the distance. It was then that I saw his hand go up. I leapt from the bushes and began a normal stride down the path. No one was around.

My pace quickened as I came nearer to my goal: the dormitories. I couldn't wait to tell e-Shack what had happened. But then it occurred to me that perhaps I shouldn't. Not yet anyway. If I was being watched, I could put my friends' lives in danger if someone thought they knew too much.

I had not been missed and just settled in to a normal evening's tasks: homework, chores, and idle chitchat. The days came and went, and I soon became proficient in code writing—memorizing the letters so as not to be seen with the coin in hand.

I wrote Moreck more about my dream with the diggers in it and asked when I might be able to come back to the hideaway in order to see what I could do to help. He did not want to risk another visit too soon and asked me to have patience. I understood, of course, but that didn't help my frustration in any way.

My only real problem since coming back was how to explain why I had suddenly started calling the dog by a new name. "Oh, it was just something that I read in one of the library scrolls and liked. Don't you think that he looks like a Zeke?" I lied.

CHAPTER 7

The Finishing Year

We had come to the end of yet another school term. Our final year was upon us. This was our time to learn all the finer points of the king's court: the proper way to eat, sit, cough, and oh yes, grovel before the greatest king on earth. We now wore the clothes of the palace soothsayers.

We no longer had the privilege of a single teacher. These first few months of our third term we were evaluated and re-evaluated. Any area that was found lacking prompted an extensive training session that could last weeks or even months. I still spent time with Sol every day, but only after being instructed in advanced areas of study that were considered more important to my coming stand before the king.

"All answers must come without thinking! They must be automatic. No hesitation is permitted before the king," our teachers repeated to us on a daily basis.

This was my eighteenth year and my body had gone through many changes since I had first arrived. I looked like a man, even if I didn't feel like one on the inside. When walking through the common areas, we were now greeted in terms of the highest respect from all the underclassmen.

I could only hope that I wasn't going to disappoint everyone by suddenly becoming completely mute on the day of our final assessment. It has always amazed me how everything can come down to just one single day, one single moment of time, one solitary chance to change your future. If we failed now, we would all slip into oblivion, lost from the great purpose that we had been brought here to achieve.

Zeke had become more than just a fur ball that ate and slept. He was now my sole contact between my waking world and a world of dreams dominated by the Ma-ji. They wanted to know everything about my nightly flight into the dreamtime. I wrote down as much as I could remember and secretly attached the coded letters beneath Zeke's heavy coat.

I could go weeks without hearing anything back. Then one day, I received an urgent note to meet Moreck.

It had been many months since our initial meeting and the trip under the falling waters of the Euphrates Maiden. This time, he wanted me to meet him outside the palace grounds. I was to take Wildfire and leave immediately upon receiving the note.

I made some excuse to the others and quickly made my way to the stables. Wildfire sensed the urgency in my demeanor. We wasted no time in getting to the desired location. I looked around, but this place seemed to be deserted.

When Moreck walked out of the darkness, I jumped. I had not even sensed a presence.

"We must go quickly," was all that he said as he turned toward Wildfire. "Back to the stables." And he slapped him on the back. He bolted from sight.

"Wildfire is too conspicuous . . . just in case you were followed," he replied before I had a chance to ask.

"But the stable hands will think something is wrong if Wildfire returns without me," I commented.

"We've taken care of that; trust me!" Moreck continued as he led me deeper into the forest undergrowth. "Here we are," he sighed, and we entered through a small opening in a large boulder.

Once inside, he began to explain the urgency of the calling. "Men have died, or at least we think they have. We can't find any trace of them. You see, the diggers have come upon something, something that you have seen in your dreams: a mask, one of the lost seven masks. We believe it to be the most important mask of all: the mask of life unending."

"But why are people dying, if it is a mask of life?" I queried.

"Exactly, that's what we wondered. There are those that feel that this mask may contain and protect the remnants of the ancient Tree of Life known to grow only in the garden of Eden itself," Moreck explained as we walked deeper into the coolness of the cave. "As I am sure you know, the way of the Tree of Life is said to be protected by swords of flaming death so that no mortals may eat of the fruit of the tree and live forever in their present carnal state. Only an enlightened soul, one that has already died to the physical, should be able to cross through the bounds of this flame."

"Then isn't this something better off left alone?" I asked, trying to understand why being eternally bound to an imperfect physical body would be a desirable state.

"Ah, yes, for you or me it would not be profitable, but there are those who work for the king and strive to bring him into an eternal reign of power and conquest—a kingdom without end." Moreck shuddered at the thought. "All things have their time, but without change there is no growth, civilization stalemates, and the soul can never be free."

"Where are we going, and what do you expect me to be able to do?" I asked tentatively.

"I am taking you to where we last saw the men. It is up to you what happens next. We down here are all out of ideas," mumbled Moreck as we both stumbled deeper into the hole.

The light was poor but more than adequate to illuminate this underground sanctuary. It was surprisingly cool and comforting, not at all what I would have expected from such confined quarters.

After many hours, our hike was ended. A large room resplendent with stalagmites and stalactites glowed from the reflection of a ring of fire located in the precise center of the cavernous hall. The stalagmites took on a ghostly glare as they danced to the flickering flames of the foreboding firelight.

Even from a distance, I could see that this fire was unlike any other that I had ever seen. The flames rotated in a perfect circle around what looked like another mask, enfolding and out-folding as they went.

And that wasn't all. I could also see the faint outlines of what looked like two men being carried along inside the ring of fire.

"How long have they been in there?" I asked as we made our way down to the others at the edge of the flame.

"Who?" Moreck replied, not understanding what I was talking about.

"I see what look like the faint images of two men in the flame, spinning around inside it like leaves caught up in a whirlwind," I continued.

Moreck then explained how none of them could look directly into the flames; to do so could mean days without sight at all. All he could tell me was that these two men had tried to cross the fire ring barrier and had disappeared, supposedly consumed by this flaming sword of protection.

The mask at the center was so close and yet so unattainable. Could the power that this mask held be so valuable as to warrant an impenetrable force to keep its secret?

Questions whirled in my mind like the fires that swirled continuously before me. Was there a way inside? Was it possible to free those trapped within a fire that had not yet consumed them—supposing that they were still alive, of course?

Time seemed to be suspended in this place. Inside the ring of fire, I could sense no yesterday or today or even a tomorrow. I instinctively knew that if I approached too closely, I would be swept up into the vortex as well, perhaps forever.

In that moment when I tried to devise a plan, the plan came to me in the form of a large vine that dropped down upon me from the roof of the cave. It must have grown from the surface, penetrating deep underground. But why did it happen to separate from the walls at just that moment?

The vine spoke to me of a way, a way into the vortex to save the two men trapped there. At that, the vine entwined itself around me, and with an almost crushing clinch, it locked itself into place, as much a part of me now as my own skin. There was only one thing left to do—walk into the fire.

My legs fought the thought. I had suffered many a nightmare about being burned alive after I was taken in the fiery conquest of my homeland invasion. I can still taste the flames of that day.

With no other option, I closed my eyes and let my body be swept up inside the ring. I was floating with no sense of up or down, left or right. It was only then that I opened my eyes.

The flames encircled me but did not touch me. As I floated in a complete void of noise, I began to notice the two men as they flew past—around and around me. I reached out my hand and grabbed one, then the other. With both hands full, however, I had no way of pulling us to freedom outside the ring.

It had seemed that we were all stuck, when the vine began to move. It disappeared into the wall of fire, but it still had a tight hold on me. Closer and closer we came to the burning wall, and then we were all thrown from the whirling mass into the shocked arms of the other diggers.

It was they who had saved us. They had pulled and pulled using the stalagmites as leverage until they freed us.

I suddenly recognized one of the men that had come from the fire: Barthalemu. He looked up at me from the cave floor and said "Thank you, kind sir. I owe you my life."

"It is Moreck that you should thank. He has left no task undone in order to bring you both back. I, like you, am confounded by what has just happened. I do not understand it any more than you," I replied, my confusion showing more with every syllable that I uttered.

"Let us leave this place quickly," Barthalemu urged.

With that, we all made our way to the closest exit and back to the hideaway chambers. This was only my second visit, but I had very much wanted to see it again, and perhaps, learn more about the Ma-ji.

"Our last visit was unavoidably brief," Barthalemu quipped as he led us toward a side chamber door. He took a large skeleton key from his pocket and inserted it noisily into the lock. After a few failed turns, the rusted door lock popped open and Barthalemu, Moreck, the second man of the fire, and myself entered single file. All others passed on by as the great door clanged shut behind us.

This room was cluttered with many scrolls and tablets, some laid out on various tables, others cast aside in heaps on the floor.

"Sorry about the mess to your office," Moreck spoke by way of an explanation to the concerned look that was now evident on Barthalemu's face. "We hoped to find in these scrolls a clue as to what had happened to you."

"I understand," Barthalemu whispered consolingly. "I will tidy up later, but for now, please be seated, all of you," he entreated. "It is important for us to understand what has just transpired. Daniel, this is Horace. He assisted me in gathering information on the dig site. He was the first to be caught up in the ring of fire."

"Hello, Horace. I am pleased to meet you," I said. But as I extended a hand of friendship, he pulled away. "Is there a problem?"

"No, no, it is just that I have never shaken the hand of such a great one. There is much speculation that you may very well be . . ." and Horace broke off as Barthalemu gave him a sideways glance.

"Ahem, enough of that. We are not here to discuss speculations. We are here to try and piece together what is happening around that mask at the dig site," Barthalemu quickly redirected the conversation. "Now, Daniel, can you tell us any more about that dream you had, the one with the diggers in it?"

I spent the next several hours explaining all I knew about the dream. The three of them listened intently and did not interrupt even a single time during my monologue.

Once finished, silence filled the room. No one spoke for several minutes as each tried to take in all that had been said. For me, however, there was nothing else to consider. But the looks on their faces seemed to indicate that there was much more to be said, only I didn't think that they were going to let me in on too much more of it just then. I was right.

It was Barthalemu who finally broke the silence. "We must get you back before anyone suspects." He looked back and forth between Horace and Moreck. He failed to meet my eyes fully as he stood to escort me from the room. As we walked toward the door, he suddenly stopped and turned to address Moreck in barely more than a whisper.

It was then that I saw it, a clay tablet in full view on one of the tables. The writing was plain as well as shocking in its content. It spoke of the mask of life unending and a Great One who would come and be able to enter and exit the flaming death at will.

I looked up from the tablet just as Barthalemu turned back toward me. I knew that it would do me no good to try and get any answers from him at this point, but maybe Moreck would not be quite as elusive later.

We all exchanged polite goodbyes as Moreck and I left the room. After what seemed like a suitable amount of quiet during our long journey back to the surface, I struggled to find the right way to begin a conversation.

"I have never seen a fire like that. How does one explain why it continues to burn and burn throughout all time?" An awkward start, yes, but my best attempt to broach the subject.

"It is believed to be the very fire of creation, always burning. This fire is one with eternity and knows not destruction but life," Moreck's words echoed through the damp halls.

Nothing else was said as we finally entered back into the realm of a fading sunset. With a quick whistle, Moreck called out, first once, then twice. Wildfire came galloping out of the gathering dusk. I was so happy to see him standing bright and eager before us.

"Go. Wildfire knows the way home from here. We will meet again soon." Moreck smiled a tentative smile as Wildfire and I sped away, racing through the ensuing darkness back to the stables.

The evening—calm with the palace torches burning brightly—was a welcome diversion from the afternoon's turmoil. But with every flame that I passed on my way back to the dormitory, I was pulled deeper into a question of flames without destruction. What could possibly protect human flesh from being consumed and turned into ashes?

Either this was an unusual flame, or something unusual provided a barrier to the heat. This would be my next task in the library, but for now, I had to catch up with what the others were doing.

As I came up the dormitory steps, I noticed Abed running back and forth between the porch and the interior study area. He did this with some great urgency. If I didn't know better, I would have thought that maybe his hair was on fire.

Upon closer inspection, I noticed a dark hairy mass closely shadowing his every hurried step—Zeke.

"What is going on here?" I yelled.

"Get him off, get him off," Abed screamed as he ran past for the third time.

"Zeke, come here!" I said, and Zeke immediately stopped chewing Abed's robes and sat down at my side. "What was that all about?"

"Nothing," Abed sneered, and quickly left the room.

Just then, Hanan and e-Shack came up the steps and entered the dormitory—both immersed in a most raucous argument.

"What is wrong with everyone tonight?" I shouted.

"Nothing. Why?" e-Shack remarked as the heated conversation immediately died down.

"How are things with you?" Hanan inquired, trying to put a pleasant face on. "We haven't seen much of you the last couple of days."

"Busy, busy, busy . . ." I repeated as I sat down at the table.

"Tell me about it," Hanan sighed as he fell exhausted into a cushy, large side chair. "I don't think that I am ever going to get past all the different things they can ask us about ancient Egypt."

"Where is Abed?" e-Shack interrupted. "I have something that you all need to hear."

"I'll go get him," I said as I wanted to check on him anyway. As I neared his room, I thought that I could hear crying.

"Abed? Are you ok? Look, e-Shack would like to talk to all of us downstairs. He says that it's really important."

"I will be right there; just give me a minute," he replied with a rather forced ease.

As I turned to go back down the stairs, I caught just the hint of a second voice coming from Abed's room. Could someone else have been here all along, hiding out? And was Abed hiding him? And if so, why?

I heard footsteps from inside the room and hurried down to rejoin the others.

"What is taking you two so long?" e-Shack sighed as Abed and I both entered the room. "I understand that the king's court will be very difficult this year. The Chaldean High Council is intent upon placing their students at the highest levels of the government. They feel that no one else can even compare to their demonstrated abilities."

"Look, we are studying as hard as we can. What else do you want us to do?" Hanan countered in a most argumentative tone.

"There is plenty we can do," e-Shack stressed. "I understand that questions will be taken from the history of Babel."

"Babel . . . we don't know anything about Babel," Abed chimed in. "How did you find out about that requirement?"

"Never mind how I found out," e-Shack asserted a little more harshly than I thought was appropriate. "Here are the manuscripts that you need to know. I will be quizzing all three of you on these over the next few months. Don't let me down!"

Now that was strange. Not just the reference to the ancient civilization of Babel, but e-Shack's distaste for being questioned by the others was very uncharacteristic.

No one stayed around to talk much after that. We all scattered to the privacy of our rooms. What was going on? Maybe the stress of finals was making everyone crack.

Zeke jumped on my bed once I entered the room. He only did this when he had a message for me. I searched the underside of his fur but found nothing. Had a message been sent and intercepted? Was that why Zeke had attacked Abed? He had never been anything but exuberant at seeing any of the four of us before.

I quickly wrote a short note, in code of course, to ask Moreck if he had just sent me a message. I tied it to Zeke's undercoat of thick fur and sent him on his way, hoping against hope that I was wrong.

CHAPTER 8

Betrayal

Our third year of class was about to come to an end, and in that time, I felt that I had somehow lost my three best friends. We had been split up in classes after the first year. And there were those times that I had the feeling they thought that I was being treated "special."

I knew something was wrong even before I sent that note to Moreck. But it was worse than that; I knew that something terrible was just about to happen. How do you prepare for something when you don't even know from which direction it will come.

I didn't have to wait long, however. The next morning, just after sunrise, soldiers arrived at our dormitory. It was from the highest level, because Arioch himself led the procession. We were all rustled from our beds and brought down to the common area.

"What is the meaning of this?" e-Shack demanded.

"Our quarrel is not with you, or you"—Arioch looked from e-Shack to Hanan—"or you." His eyes lingered upon Abed. Abed looked only at the floor in front of him. "We have come for you, Daniel." Shock filled the room. "You have been accused of companioning with the enemies of Babylon."

I was led away in shackles before all my classmates—
as classes were about to commence, all students had
gathered on the grounds outside. Whispers spread
throughout the assembly.

I was brought before the Chaldean High Council to be
charged with my crime. Once inside the chambers, Arioch
led me to a high platform at the very center of a vast circular
room. The person in charge wasted no time in beginning
the proceedings.

"You have been summoned before this council to face
the most severe accusation of companioning with the
enemies of Babylon," he read from a small scroll. "What do
you have to say for yourself?"

"I . . . I . . ." At a complete loss for words, I stammered,
not knowing what to say, when . . .

"Who is this man? We are in the midst of a trial," the
magistrate demanded.

I turned my head and noticed e-Shack come from behind
me to approach the bench. "I am Daniel's counsel," he
began. "According to Chaldean law, an accused is
permitted counsel once formal charges have been made
against him."

"Is this man your counsel?" the frustrated magistrate
asked of me.

"Yes," was the only other word I ever said at that hearing.

For you see, e-Shack was most well versed in the laws
of the Babylonian Empire. I had not thought too much
about this until now. Nor had I appreciated it as much as I
did at that very moment.

"Who has brought these most serious of charges against
this man?" e-Shack bellowed with a most forceful voice.
"Let the accusers be brought before this council and present
their evidence for all in the realm to hear."

The magistrate, looking as though he had just lost the
wind from his sails, motioned to a side door where stepped

out a woman that I had only seen occasionally while visiting the library.

"What do you know of this man?" the magistrate asked the woman.

The woman would not look up at me, and her words showed much strain at their delivery. She spoke of seeing me on several occasions talking to a man known to belong to a secret sect—all secret societies had been outlawed years before.

The magistrate called another and another to testify against me. When finally, the most damaging witness of all was brought in—Abed. e-Shack and I both gazed openmouthed at the sight. How could this be?

"You are a friend of the accused, are you not?" a maniacal look came upon the magistrate's face.

"Yes, sir . . . we are among the captives from Axios."

"And what evidence do you have to bring before this council?"

I heard very little of what the magistrate said after that, not understanding why or how Abed could do what it now appeared he was doing.

"I have this," and he pulled out of his robes a scroll that I recognized immediately as the kind Moreck would send.

Abed's eyes never met mine, but I could tell that it pained him greatly to say the words that he spoke. I could only hope that the council did not yet know how to decipher the writing on the scroll.

The magistrate took the scroll and announced to the room that this was proof positive that I was involved in a forbidden society.

"These markings belong to the ancient sect known as the Ma-ji. How do you, Daniel, explain why they were found attached to the fur on the underside of your dog?" The magistrate concluded his arguments and released all the witnesses.

Quickly regaining his composure, e-Shack began his best rebuttal. "There is no evidence that Daniel has done anything against the kingdom. He has been an exemplary student and has always shown the utmost regard for the law."

"Enough," yelled the magistrate. "We are not unreasonable. It is therefore our decision that Daniel be locked in the lion's den from sunset this very day until the sun arises on the morrow. If he is innocent, as you claim, no harm will come to him; the gods will deliver him without a scratch. But if he is truly guilty of this high crime, he will be devoured and justice will indeed be served. Take him away!"

The magistrate would hear no more supplication from e-Shack on this matter. I was doomed. I was taken to a cell and clothed in the attire of a criminal. They did let me, as a condemned man, have visitors until my last hour. Hanan and e-Shack both sat with me until they were forced out.

Abed would not leave his room, but still I could hold no ill will against him. For what he had done, he must have had a good enough reason. I had to trust in that.

At exactly sunset, they came.

In complete silence, I was led from the cell down a long and narrow hallway, down two flights of stairs, and then another. All too soon, we stood before the very gates of hell.

The outer gate was opened and only one guard and I entered into the small area between the gates. The outer gate closed, the guard moved to open the inner gate.

I walked stoically forward, or at least I tried to. There were, after all, worse things than being eaten by a lion. But at the moment, I couldn't thing of a single thing that made this situation feel any better.

It was dark, completely dark inside the lion's den. I had no idea where the lion was or how it might choose to attack.

I stood by the door staring into the darkened chamber waiting, and waiting . . . but nothing ever happened.

Maybe the lion wasn't particularly hungry right now, I thought. I could hear breathing, heavy breathing, being echoed through the small chamber. Turning toward the source of this consternation, my eyes slowly began to open to a huge figure lying on the floor not ten feet from where I now stood.

Could it be? . . . no! A lion of enormous size, to be sure, but not just any lion; this was the lion that I had freed some year and a half ago when trapped in the maze. I held his life in my hand that day, and it now appeared that my life was being held in equal jeopardy.

Instinctively, I moved as far to the other side of the cell as possible. My back against the wall, I slid down the cool moist stones and sat squarely on the floor, still staring at the far corner. This was the waiting game.

I wondered if he perhaps remembered me. I wondered if it made any difference if he remembered me or not. I wondered how many more hours it would be until sunrise.

Somewhere in the night, our standoff fell away, and I slumped over into an unsettled sleep. If I was going to be eaten, I at least didn't want to be awake for the whole thing.

It felt like a rough wet sponge being rubbed over my right arm and then up onto my face, over and over again it came. I was lost in a dream, far from the palace in a lush green pasture. Zeke was with me, and at first, I thought that it was he that meant to lavish his affection upon me, but then, I realized . . . I am not outside—even though a bright shaft of light hit me squarely in the face. For a brief moment, I tried to work out what was happening. The last thing that I remembered was staring at that lion in the opposite corner, but I couldn't see anything in the opposite corner now.

Oh no, where was he?

And what happened to that hard, cold floor?

Both questions were answered in an instant, for you see, I was now lying on that very lion, and it was his tongue that I felt waking me to the sunrise. I wasn't afraid—shocked at first—but not afraid.

Sunrise! That meant that the guard should be coming soon to release me from the cell, but I was in no hurry. I was most comfortable and quite warm.

My friend e-Shack was with the guard, who came to a clanging of the keys. Timidly e-Shack called, "Daniel? Daniel? Oh please be alive!"

"Keep your shirt on," I replied. "Did you doubt that I would not be delivered? And without a single scratch, I must add, although I am a bit stiff from sleeping on that hard floor. Thank goodness they put this lion in here to keep me warm."

I saw e-Shack's mouth fall open, and the guard stumbled backward when they saw me still lying wrapped around the lion's mane.

"Don't worry! We're old friends. I want to make sure that this lion is well taken care of and is released from this hold as soon as possible," I commented as I walked past both of them out of the dungeon.

CHAPTER 9

Brothers

E-Shack and I walked solemnly back toward the dormitories. He didn't seem to know what to make of finding me alive.

Upon entering our quarters, I came face-to-face with Hanan and Abed. You would have thought that they had seen someone who had just risen from the dead. Neither of them looked like they had slept all night.

Abed immediately hugged my neck and sobbed, begging for forgiveness.

"I hold nothing against you that you need to be forgiven for," I explained. "You did what you thought was right, and for that you need never apologize."

"You could have been killed by that lion. All because I believed them when they told me you were plotting against the king." Abed's voice trembled. "What's been going on? Why do you keep sneaking off?"

He was right, of course. I should have trusted my best friends to understand and not to keep so much from them. After that, I began to explain all about how I had met Moreck and been taken to the secret hideaway of the Ma-ji.

We talked for hours as I poured my soul out to them. They three listened intently to my every word, but on coming to the end of my saga, I noticed Hanan glance sideways at e-Shack as if asking permission for something.

Then e-Shack nodded his approval to Hanan, and with my mouth still open, I began to learn that I was not the only one involved in intrigue and danger. How could I have been so self-absorbed as not to notice what was going on right under my very nose?

Hanan moved closer, and in a hushed tone, said, "Remember that first time that you vanished, under the Euphrates Maiden? Well, that very night, we had a strange visitor. He came rapping upon our door and seemed scared that anyone might notice him come to us."

And then e-Shack broke in, "This man, half hidden under a hooded robe, revealed his face once inside, and a familiar face it was too. Remember the man that I told you I met while on a school field trip. Well, it was none other than him."

Hanan cut in again. "He told e-Shack and me a tale of impending crisis about to seize the kingdom. The king himself would be led astray by one of his own trusted advisors. He would then become consumed with arrogance and pride at the knowledge that his kingdom was the greatest of all time, surpassing all those that had gone before, and all those yet to come."

Abed came suddenly to life at this point. "It was then that I, having been sound asleep upstairs, suddenly became aware of a strange voice whispering somewhere outside my door. I crept to the landing and overheard just the last portion of this man's harrowing story. Suddenly realizing that they might not be alone, e-Shack hushed the man, and I could hear him advance upon the landing. Quickly, I returned to my room and pretended to be fast asleep. I heard e-Shack close the door as silently as possible, and his footfalls faded. I heard nothing else of the conversation with the stranger. So that's all I knew was secrets, secrets, secrets, from all of you."

Excitedly, e-Shack took over the telling once again: "I came back downstairs just in time to see the stranger whisper a few final words into Hanan's ear before he sped out the door, hood firmly back over his face. Hanan and I stood staring for a few moments with confused looks into questioning eyes, both his and mine."

"Wait, wait, wait. Are you saying that each of you heard only a portion of what the man said?" I asked.

"Yes. I guess that would be true," Hanan answered as if to realize this for the very first time.

"All right, let's see if I can't piece this together," I said as I had heard quite enough to know why things had fallen into such a sad state. "Mysterious goings-on by me and add in a stranger here and there, cramming for final exams, and too much secrecy between brothers, and you have a fertile ground for treachery."

We talked well into the afternoon before finally coming to an agreement. Trust, amongst ourselves, would be the only way we would survive in this new land. Hand upon hand upon hand upon hand, the four of us pledged our honors to each other, for good or for bad.

The next few weeks I was still piecing things together from their point-of-view. It had been our very first year at Babylon when Arioch had the occasion to introduce me personally to the king. Nebuchadnezzar was a man who always liked to be up on every issue relating to the kingdom, and every issue seemed to relate to the kingdom somehow—including me.

At the time, I did not think much of my friends not having had the same introduction. As a matter of fact, they still had not personally met the king when I was thrown into the lion's den. By our second year, I had seen him no less than five times. I probably did go on about it a bit too much. It is so easy to get an inflated view of yourself when you are sharing the king's table and others are not.

Now where was I, oh yes, we were about to finish our third and final year as students in the scholastic confines of Chaldean academia. Our heads were chocked full of all sorts of supposedly "meaningful" facts. I did not think that my head could have held one more fact as the last day before we stood before the king came to a close.

That night in the dormitories was a frightful one. Abed was walking in circles around the table muttering to himself, waving off anyone who dared to speak to him. Hanan and e-Shack just sat gazing mindlessly into the stars from the porch, and I, not knowing what else to do, decided to go for a walk around the grounds.

Solitude always worked best for me during times of testing. I found a quiet spot off the main path, sat down, and proceeded to clear my mind. The air was sweet and the breeze gentle upon my skin. I sat for what felt like hours. As I made to prepare my path back and try to find some sleep, I noticed some words scribbled in the dirt: good luck tomorrow. I should have suspected; the Ma-ji always seemed to know my rising up and sitting down with an uncanny foreknowledge.

I wiped the words away and headed back to the now darkened rooms of the dorm.

The next day, we four stood as brothers before the king. The different classes were each giving a unique standard that was to be raised high into the air if someone in that group dared to try and answer a question put forth by the king. It seemed easy enough—One question, one answer. We soon learned, however, that incomplete answers, and especially wrong answers, received severe point penalties.

This type of test did not single out any one individual. It rather emphasized certain military-style cohesions within the groups. Everyone in a group had to answer at least one question before anyone else could step forward to answer a second question. This really hurt those groups where only one person had put forth the effort to learn the material.

It could not have been better for us, however; e-Shack understood the legal aspects, Hanan the historical accountings, Abed the agricultural, and I, governmental affairs. No man stands alone, and on this very special day, we learned how each of us had a very special part to play. None was any more important than the other.

At the end of it all, not only had we graduated, we had been ranked as the top group out of all the classes. So much better were we than the others that our entire group was selected to fill positions working as "ministers-in-training" directly under the king. To say that there weren't several people very unhappy about this would be an understatement. We were making more enemies by the day, but at least for now, the brothers four were inseparable.

CHAPTER 10

The Underling

J ust when we were getting used to being senior in life, we were all bumped back to junior grade slime once again, reduced to getting refreshments and holding the towel for those senior to us. All a part of life, I suppose, but I couldn't help but think that we were being treated with a little more disdain than was normal.

It was then that I met Kira. She was totally unremarkable, as I remember. Nothing stood out about her. Nothing gave anyone cause for a second glance; perhaps that is why she was chosen for the duties she held. That job was as a special envoy of the king and his family. She would ensure that all their mundane day-to-day needs were met.

Silently working in the background of every function, she had access to every room in the palace, and maybe more importantly, the king's ear.

The day that I met her, I was wandering aimlessly, lost in the never-ending underground maze that lay beneath the entire palace complex. To say that I was lost may be an overstatement. One could always climb the many stairways to the surface to re-orient oneself, but that was both time-consuming and exhausting.

Since the maze was deliberately left unmarked, and there were many hidden staircases, I was resigned to wandering about until I found an exit close to where I thought I needed to be.

Kira came to my rescue.

Appearing suddenly out of what just before had been a solid wall, she paused, considered me intently, then approached cautiously.

"Are you lost?" she asked.

"I suppose so," was my reply.

"Where are you trying to go?"

"I am on my way to the magistrate's chambers. I thought that I could save some time by cutting through down here, but . . ."

"Follow me," she entreated, cutting me off without further explanation. "You were almost there, but you would never have seen the entrance to the stairwell unless you knew exactly where to look."

Pushing just the right stone, the wall opened with the ease of piece of wood gliding upon the water. I thanked her heartily and hurried on my way, entering the magistrate's chambers behind a large hanging tapestry.

From that moment on, I became increasingly aware of how often and in how many different places I saw Kira. She always smiled a soft smile when our eyes met, an indication that both confirmed and encouraged our friendship. I would often make some excuse to step away from the others around the room just to see how she was doing.

Since graduating, we four had been moved to new quarters. The dormitory life was long gone. Our new home was representative of the high stature that had been placed upon us. The one-room bedroom with the small courtyard patio became a huge multiroom complex with panoramic views of the palace grounds and beyond.

New areas were opened to us within the realm, and new responsibilities were added almost on a daily basis. In many respects, training was never really ever over, but we could not devote as much time to formal studies as we had previously.

Sol had taken over the instruction of new charges, but we did stay in close contact by exchanging short notes sent via the palace messenger system.

As for Moreck and the Ma-ji, notes, even encrypted ones, were no longer safe for communicating. We had to find a new way to evade the many ears and eyes of the palace.

The solution to this dilemma was, I must say, most unusual—fire. The many furnaces that supplied the palace with hot water burned night and day and were never extinguished. While walking around one of the larger furnaces, I noticed more than just the crackling of flames as they consumed their fuel. It sounded like many voices, familiar voices.

"Moreck?" I called into the flame. "Is that you?"

"Daniel! We have been trying every way we know to reach you since the trial. We were glad to hear that lions find you most distasteful. We thought that we had lost you for sure."

"I am still here, but how can I hear you through this fire?"

"Not really sure, but there seems to be some connection between where you are and the flames that surround the mask of life unending; that's where we are now."

"Is it secure on your end?" interrupted Barthalemu.

"Yes," I whispered—not quite knowing why I felt the need to whisper. "No one ever comes down to the bottom of the furnace; it is supplied from the topside. I only find myself here because I was trying to find yet another shortcut through the underground maze."

"Good, the fates are with us. Let us use this method of communicating for now. Always stagger your visits— nothing scheduled or too predictable from your end. I will station someone around the flame here twenty-four hours a day. Now get going before you are discovered."

Get going I did, but I still had to be very aware of how to get back to this place. The nice thing about the maze was that it was almost impossible to follow someone without being seen. I felt, at the time, that I had found the perfect connection with the Ma-ji.

It still took me a while before I finally found my way back to the surface from the maze. I wanted to be sure that I understood all the possible ways of getting to the furnace floor without getting lost again.

Once back in my quarters, I heard e-Shack singing at the top of his lungs, and it wasn't pretty. All four of us lived within close proximity. And that had its good points and its bad points. I could only assume that all this noise was a good thing and hurried down to e-Shack's quarters.

"What are you doing?" I yelled through the opened door.

"Oh, Daniel. So good to see you, my friend," e-Shack chortled. "Great news. One of the king's advisors saw me at your trial and wants me to be his underling. Isn't that great? He is the most respected man in his field."

"His underling . . . you are happy about being someone's underling?" I responded crassly.

"No, you don't understand!" e-Shack continued, "only once every twenty-five years is someone chosen for an opportunity as grand as this, and now it's me . . . it's me . . . can you believe it?"

"Yeah, I suppose. So when do you start?" I was trying to be happy for him.

"First thing in the morning. I meet his staff just after sunrise. Oh, this is so great . . ."

I left e-Shack still humming and dancing about. I don't think that he even noticed that I had gone. Now to check on Abed and Hanan—it was always my habit to see how they all were on a daily basis.

Hanan wasn't around, probably at the library. That is where he usually was to be found. Abed, however, was right where I would have expected to find him, lying face down on the bed scribbling furiously on a scroll of parchment. He had been assigned to the agricultural ministry and he was working up charts for some newly discovered plant compounds.

"How's it going there, Abed?" I asked as I flopped down on the bed beside him.

"Be careful! You are going to make me spill my ink . . . Arioch came looking for you earlier. He wanted to talk to you as soon as you got back," Abed rattled off without answering my question.

"Where is he?"

"He said he would be working late. He's probably still over at his work quarters."

I bounced up off the bed—Abed scrambling to catch scrolls and an ink well that was sent careening—and headed for Arioch's workplace. The lamps were still lighted when I arrived, but no Arioch.

Scuttling about, waiting for Arioch to return, I noticed a large manuscript lying under some scrolls on the desk. Casually, as if looking for a writing instrument, I moved the scrolls back just enough to make out the title—A History of the Ma-ji.

Suddenly, approaching footsteps forced me to once again cover the manuscript title and leap to the other side of the room so as not to raise suspicion.

"Ah, Daniel, here you are," Arioch called out as he entered the room. "I need to talk with you about a future campaign that we are considering."

I don't believe that I have mentioned what my assignment was once I left school. I was put in the department of soothsaying and magician studies. The king was very interested in the future, especially predicting it correctly beforehand. Sol had been grooming me personally for just this role during the last two years of my schooling.

"Can you take a look at this scroll listing our plans to meet the Egyptians later this month? Let me know if you see anything or dream on the matter within the next couple of days."

Arioch left me to pore through the documents laid out on his desk. "Put out the lamps when you are done. I have another appointment and must be on my way. See you tomorrow," his voice faded as he pushed through the closed door on his way out.

My typical method of gathering information about a future event was to read as much as possible about the proposed engagement and then to sleep on it for a few days. If nothing caused me deep distress in my dreams, I would figure that the event was benign.

Right now, however, my thoughts were more concentrated on the manuscript at the bottom of the large pile I was now supposed to be sorting through.

"Where did he get this manuscript?" I whispered to myself. I had been looking for any kind of written information about the Ma-ji for the better part of two years and found nothing but a few snippets.

"Had he deliberately left it here knowing that I would find it, and perhaps, read it?" I further wondered.

Well, read it I did. The volume was huge, and I knew there was not time to read if from the beginning, so I opened it and perused the compactly written pages looking for something that might grab my attention.

I didn't have to read long; somewhere in the middle section, I came across the words " . . . eternal life to all that drink of this living water . . ." There was a sketch of a small child holding a basin in both hands, her innocent-looking face gazing contentedly into the pool of water.

There was something familiar about this child. I had seen her before, but had it been in my dreams or somewhere else?

Hours had slipped by before I realized my time was all but gone. I had to get back.

What did all this mean? Whereas the Tree of Life was blocked and forbidden to humanity, this "living water" was being freely offered to anyone that chose to drink of it. Now, how to find it . . .

That night a dream formed in me. An all-encompassing consciousness revealed itself in the form of a nighthawk. I flew alongside his powerful wings and saw the earth fall away as we rose into the sky.

We flew into the sunset over innumerable fields and pastures, finally landing in an ancient olive tree; its branches old and twisted, hung low to the ground, weary of age and time's ceaseless onslaught.

"Where are we? Why are we here?" I asked.

"Listen with your eyes, see with your ears, and you shall know the where and the why," was his only response.

I looked, but saw nothing. It was not until I heard them that I could see their true identity: apparitions in the wind, fluid of form and barely apparent. There were two, between which a dance ensued. The melody was poetic and subdued in its ovation. Each, in turn, yielded and gave of itself to the other.

The dance continued for some time. Just as I was about to remove my eyes from this scene, the music changed; the colors became dark and foreboding. As one figure bowed at the final intonation of music, it happened.

A sword appeared from the hidden recesses of the many-layered garment that the first figure wore and struck a fatal blow to the still-bowing second figure.

I now knew where we were: the meeting location with the Egyptian council. And I also knew why we were there: to stop a murder. But still, something was not right. I later realized that what had passed itself off as the Egyptian councilman was, in fact, an imposter. I supposed that his intent was to provoke war between Babylon and Egypt. This was not to be a betrayal by the Egyptians at all.

Arioch was informed of these matters just prior to his departure.

"Maybe, you can arrive in such a fashion as to prevent the Egyptian council from being ravaged," I advised Arioch. "Be careful; let nothing happen to our delegation or to you."

Arioch smiled his trademark smile, shook his head, saluted, and rode away. Twenty-five horsemen accompanied him, and as I watched them depart, I was reminded once again (Sol's wisdom) that knowing one possible future could never change the very dynamic nature that it will always be. In other words, when one version of the future is changed, no one can be truly confident that the alternative is somehow better.

With Arioch now gone, it suddenly occurred to me that I would have as much time as I wanted to read the Ma-ji manuscript. I hurried back to our work chambers to continue my research. Where could it be? It was no longer on the desk. Had he put it away somewhere?

I searched and searched—to no avail. At this point, I started to consider the possibility that the manuscript was never really there at all. Arioch would not keep something as important as that from me, knowing my insatiable interest in the Ma-ji.

Finding nothing to hold my interest further in the office, I headed for the furnace, and perhaps, a long talk with Moreck or Barthalemu.

"ARE YOU THERE?" I wailed.

"What are you trying to do, scare me to death?" It was none other than Moreck on the other side.

"Sorry about that, but I am glad you're there," I sighed in relief. "I need to talk to someone about this passage that I read in a manuscript entitled A History of the Ma-ji. I found it in Arioch's office yesterday and could only read a portion of it. Today, it's gone."

"I know of the manuscript that you speak of," Moreck affirmed. "It is relatively basic. I wouldn't worry about not having been able to view more of it; you know most of it anyway. What part of it caught your eye?"

"What do the words 'eternal life to all those that drink of this living water' mean? And there was a picture of a child holding a basin, but I know that I have seen that image before. I just don't understand why the Tree of Life is protected under threat of death for anyone trying to obtain its fruit and yet the 'living water' is free to any who would choose to drink of it," I said.

"I understand your quandary," Moreck stated. "Think of this from the standpoint of that which is taken as opposed to that which is received. You will understand all this in time. Before I forget it, I must ask you if you have seen anything of a tower in your dreams? There are those here—gifted in dreams like yourself—that see on a nightly basis, a huge tower rising up out of the earth. Its power extends to the heavens and no goal is beyond its reach. Anything like that on your end?"

"No. What do you think is going on?"

"Don't know," Moreck replied with uncertainty oozing from his every word. "See what you can find out about it there. Now get going; it's late. Until next time . . ."

And with that, I was off.

CHAPTER 11

The Great Tower

A great tower! It was well known that Babylon was built upon the ancient foundations of the fabled "Tower of Babel." Could these dreams be rising up from the very ground under our feet? And if they were, why now?

The next few weeks, my dreams gave form to a large structure rising out of the earth. A tower, yes, but it was much more than that. It had a distinctive shape, like a large statue. I could not make out its features, but I marveled at the colossal size of it.

Arioch was still on a distant frontier, meeting with the Egyptians. I could only hope that things were going well. The journey there and back would take them at least a month plus however long the meetings took.

I kept busy with my many other duties, and of course, trying to find out as much as I could about the tower. There were dozens of manuscripts written about the great civilization of Babel, and I spent many a long day reading well into the night.

I uncovered a time when mankind, speaking a common language, worked together to build great cities. They did not fight or use their power to destroy. The greatest of all these cities was to be Babel.

They had found a way to harness the knowledge of the ages, and in doing so, had gathered together all twelve of the masks of life. The ancient Ma-ji had assisted them in this venture, believing that mankind had finally come to a point of development that would bring with it a lasting peace and an unbridled stateliness for all living things.

The twelve masks would impart wisdom on a scale never before imagined. The masks were to be positioned around the city in a great circle. There were four main masks positioned at the four poles: north, south, east, and west. All others were to be placed on the circle between these main points—two between each.

Once the circle was complete, the city inhabitants would increase in understanding and communication, and the tower would rise to the heavens.

But something went wrong. There were two masks that were out of place: the east and the west. This had the effect of boosting man's ego to the point of arrogance. With the tower head nearly complete, they began to turn their attention to who would rule the city, who would take credit for this greatest achievement of all time.

Bickering took the place of cooperation, and soon the city was abandoned. The world split into a thousand different shards, each left in isolation to develop its own unique language and culture.

Only the Ma-ji stayed in the vast city. They set about to hide, move, or disguise the masks as best they could. A pact was made between them so that no one group should know the whereabouts of all the masks. Each of the four existing groups at the time would only know where four of the masks could be found. This allowed for some overlap but did not compromise the main goal of preventing a single individual to betray all.

Over the years, the Ma-ji groups dispersed or simply died off so that now only a handful were left who had retained the ancient secrets of the past Ma-ji masters.

Therefore, no remaining group, or individual for that matter, currently knew where all the masks had been hidden. That was why they were looking for someone who could enter the dreamtime and bring back the lost knowledge of the ages—me.

A tall order for anyone, I must confess. And to add to my quandary, I needed the discernment of an owl in order to know whom to trust with whatever revelation might come.

I shared this all with e-Shack, Hanan, and Abed. Having learned our lesson from before about secrets between brothers, we shared all our concerns. So too did I relay the information to Moreck via the fire of the furnace. He was most interested and suggested that we needed another meeting; there were sketches that his men had drawn that he wanted me to see.

We could not risk another meeting at the hideaway, however, so Moreck decided that he would send someone (unknown as a member of Ma-ji) to meet with me at the main library around noon the next day.

The code phase "as clever as a fox" would be used to identify the man to me. He would drop some scrolls, and I was to help him retrieve them. Only I was to retrieve more than just the scrolls in return.

The next day, I headed out to the library early. I did not want to risk being late. I found an out-of-the-way spot in a quiet corner and began to look busy studying. I had several manuscripts on my desk and was prepared to drop whatever I had in my hands at the time.

I waited and waited, always aware of the comings and goings of those around me. Nothing happened. The hours came and went with nothing more suspicious happening than a librarian toppling over a large cart of scrolls that were to be re-catalogued. Finally, the last rays of sunlight crept across the floor and out of sight. It was closing time.

What had gone wrong? I pondered. Where was the man now?

I picked up the few scrolls that I had not gotten to yet and signed them out for the evening. It hadn't been a total loss; I had learned plenty about the tower, even seen some dimensions for its overall size.

As I walked absentmindedly down the front steps, still trying to read just a bit more . . . CRASH! A man running along the pathway had come careening into me like some runaway cart.

"Sorry, so sorry, my good man. I didn't see you there; just remembered it's my wife's birthday—have to get to the shops before they close, you know, got to be clever as a fox these days . . . to stay out of trouble with the wife, I mean."

He helped me pick up the scrolls that had gone flying from my grasp and continued his hurried pace toward the plaza of merchants.

It wasn't until I returned to my quarters that I noticed that I had more than what I left the library with. "Clever as a fox"—it had happened so suddenly that I did not even know the transfer had occurred.

Excitedly, I unrolled the new scroll.

"Blank . . . it can't be blank!" I said to myself.

Well, I would have to wait a few days to find out what I needed to do in order to reveal what was written; couldn't risk going back to the furnace tonight. I disappointedly turned my attention to the other scrolls. "Let's see . . . where was I? Oh, yes, section 9, something about the head of the statue."

As I read further, I could not believe my eyes. The head of the statue was to be the crowning glory of not just a statue, but also a civilization. A crystal, chosen especially for its unique resonance, was to be placed in the elaborate headdress. Each mask, when precisely pointed toward the center of the circle, would then "come to life . . ." No, that wasn't the proper translation, " . . . bring life" to all those who dwell within its essence.

A spring of "living waters" would bubble up from the bare ground and give "life without end" to all that drink of it.

First, I learned about a Tree of Life, forbidden for humanity to eat thereof. Now, I was learning of water so refreshing as to give life unending. Could it be that, perhaps, the Tree of Life was no more magical than any other tree? Maybe it was and had always been the water that nourished the tree as it grew.

"Each is to drink of that water in turn and not to steal life from another that has previously found the source," the scroll read. This made perfect sense. I completed the reading and rereading of the scrolls before finding e-Shack in his room and informing him of what I had learned.

He listened, then replied, "Very nice."

Not at all the reaction that I had anticipated.

"What do you mean very nice?"

"Well," he began slowly, "it's not like there's a fountain of youth bubbling up in the back yard, is there? I mean, this is all very nice, but I would think that even you could see that it is mere fable, tales told by old men in order to amuse the young ones."

As I reluctantly rose to leave the room, e-Shack buried his nose back into his work. Maybe he doesn't understand the importance, or maybe he has never believed in such things. It was at times like these that I realized how little I really knew about him.

My sleep was very disturbed that night. The little girl holding the basin of water appeared over and over again, from all different angles. I tried to see something around the figure that would give me a clue as to the whereabouts, but nothing looked familiar.

I had to put this out of my mind; I had to concentrate on the tower. Something was about to happen, and I must understand what.

Several days later, Arioch returned.

"How was your trip?" I asked guardedly.

"Well, I am still alive, aren't I?"

"I mean, did things play out the way that I had predicted?"

"Yes," he began, "and then some . . ."

He told me the story of a long and dusty journey and finding an old man along the way. "This man recounted a highly decorated Egyptian army moving through the area. They were forceful and demanded to know when the Babylonian council would come."

Arioch always had a knack for keeping a person's rapt attention when telling of any campaign.

"The Egyptian assembly was just as you had described, not Egyptian at all. Dressed in the attire of the Egyptian army, they had set out to destroy our council once we were within their grasp. Knowing what to expect and learning from the old man where we could find the supposed Egyptian army, I split our forces in two just like we did at the river on our journey from Axios. The larger of the two groups circled around behind the deceptive force while a smaller band, led by me, would engage them from the front.

"It was great. We played right into their hands. They were most gracious but hardly convincing as representatives of the Egyptian realm. In short order, they wooed us into their greedy clutches.

"Once we were ensnared, they played their hand and made a move to lay waste to us all. It was then that the second group, having secretly encircled the lot, charged in and took control—and just in time too!

"Our only regret is that we did not arrive in time to save the real Egyptian forces. We found their bodies decaying in the harsh sun just a few days later. We buried them as best as we could and sent a representative back to Egypt to explain what had happened. I can only hope that they believe us."

"Does this mean that war with the Egyptians is coming?" I responded dejectedly.

"You tell me; you're the seer, after all. I must make my report to the king. I will talk to you later."

Arioch performed a sharp military turn and left the confines of the small room that we called an office.

Chapter 12

A New Tower Rises

Don't get the wrong idea about the ability to interpret dreams. I wasn't the only one who laid claim to that special gift; there were many others—soothsayers, they were called. Theirs was a select set who stayed close to the king and provided much advice, and not always to the edification of the hearer.

It is not that they lied per se. They would leave certain things out, if the occasion called for it. As the most trusted of advisors to the king, they had found that degrees of manipulation were possible when it came to highly controversial issues.

I was caught in the crosshairs on many a matter of state concern. Usually, I lost. I was only one man, while they, hearing with many ears, would speak with only one voice.

The king had found me, well, amusing but had taken no consolation in any words that I spoke before him. That was all about to change.

Just as I was not the only one concerned with dream interpretation, I was not the only one with dreams of my own. One starless night, when the moon was full and its light outshone all other celestial bodies, the king's usually tranquil sleep was disturbed by a monstrous vision.

He saw a great figure spring up from the deepest regions of the earth, pushing its way into the sunlight. It appeared to sprout from nothingness into being. Rising high into the air, it dwarfed all the other structures around it. It stood tall with feet of clay and iron, legs of bronze, a breastplate of silver, and was topped with a headdress covered in pure gold.

The sun's rays illuminated the tower in such a way as to refract the light like a finely cut jewel. And in its headdress was a large crystal chard, which cast a rainbow from the head of the great statue to the ground some sixty feet away.

Nebuchadnezzar watched as the tower—this warrior statue crafted of precious metals—began to sink under the weight of its own enormous bulk. It had stood so stately and for so long. Multitudes had gone up into its heights and peered impressively from the tower's gigantic eyes.

How could such a magnificent creation of man be thrown to the dust and consumed in such a short timeframe? he thought. And with that forlorn image still in his mind, he wept great tears of sadness.

Upon waking from this dream, Nebuchadnezzar's recollection failed him. He could not remember the sights that his eyes had seen. He could only sense the great sadness that he had felt at the dream's conclusion.

A ravenous hunger to regain his lost vision consumed him from that very hour. Immediately, he arose and summoned his trusted advisors to his side.

"I have seen a vision in my dreams of a most terrible thing. I must know what it means."

The soothsayers, still groggy from being awakened so urgently in the middle of the night, stammered amongst themselves as they tried to make out what was being requested of them.

"What troubles the great king of all the world, and what comfort may we offer his majesty this very night?" the soothsayers implored.

The king began to recount all he could remember of his lost dream and the anguish that its faded memory now posed him. "Tell me the dream and divulge the meaning that I may find rest over this matter?" he commanded resolutely.

As the soothsayers fumbled for words, a rage ignited inside the king's mind. "You don't know, do you? All these years, you have just been telling me what I want to hear."

"Oh, king, if you will only tell us your dream, we would be most obliging in delivering the meaning."

"If you were true seers, you would not only be able to tell me the interpretation of my dream, but the very dream itself. If, however, you are charlatans and liars, you will not be able to deliver to me the dream, and all your kind within the realm shall be imprisoned from this day forward.

"Guards, guards!" Nebuchadnezzar called, "take them away to prison. Round them all up and deliver them to the jailer before this day is through."

Now the simple fact of the matter was that I was also a seer, and therefore, subject to the same fate as were all the others. Arioch, knowing this, came quietly to my sleeping chambers to inform me of the king's decree before his guards could come for me.

He roused me from my slumber and explained what had transpired just a few short hours before. "You must escape before they come for you too," he sighed grievously.

"I would not know where to go, what to do—no. There must be a better way." We both sat in stunned silence trying to figure some way to rectify this dire situation.

"Let me talk to the king personally," I finally said.

"What will you say? You'll never get past the guards," Arioch shouted as I jumped from the bed and began to dress.

"I will . . . I will, if you escort me in."

With little time to put together a proper plan of action, we hurried to the palace meeting hall where Nebuchadnezzar always received his councilmen. Guards blocked our way, but the king, hearing the ruckus outside the great doors, burst through to see what was happening.

"What's going on here? Why have these men forced their way . . ." At that moment, he recognized Arioch, then turned his eyes toward me. "Daniel, why are . . ." He stopped in midsentence and stared, warily at first, and then a ray of hope seemed to spread across his wearied brow. He held up a single hand to wave off the guards. "Come with me."

We followed the king into the meeting hall, but we did not stop there. I glanced quickly at Arioch with a question on my lips. He shook it off, and we three walked on past the king's outer quarters and right on into his most private sanctum—his bedroom.

Only when we had all entered and the servant had closed the door upon us did he turn to address us once more. "I sense that you have a keen awareness that might provide a resolution to this unpleasantness. The others have always seemed too quick with an answer, too willing to provide a rational report before the king. I, more than any other, realize that so much in this world cannot be explained by reason alone. That is why I have brought you here," he pointed toward the bed.

The king looked from me to the bed—still disheveled from the night's unsettling vision. "Go ahead. Walk to this side and place your hands where my head lay this past night. I see in you the gift, still underdeveloped, but nevertheless vibrant and alive."

I am sure that my mouth was open, words bubbling to get out, but rather than to speak, I did as the king directed and walked to the side of the bed where he always slept. With another movement of his hand, he commanded me to proceed.

Unsure of what I was to do, I stretched out both hands and placed them just above the hollow of his pillow. What happened next, I can only tell you by the words of Arioch, conveyed to me later after I regained consciousness.

He told me that I went into some kind of dream state— no longer conscious, but also not asleep. I recounted the dream, image by image, while the king, eyes shut tightly, nodded his recollection of each scene.

Together, we had found a way into the recesses of a lost vision and brought it back to the light.

The king's countenance had changed to such a joy that all who beheld him from that day marveled. The days that followed were filled with mirth, and merriment sat lightly upon the hearts of all the palace workers. I even noticed Kira singing as she went about her daily duties.

The soothsayers were freed, but none ever again held the king's favor to the same extent as I did. As the months went by, I found myself increasingly in the company of the king's court, more as a friend than as an official.

The tower became the king's obsession. He called for historians, architects, and builders to study the matter so that he might know how to build such a colossal structure. There were experts on Babel and the lost twelve masks of life. They researched the exact location of the previous tower and sought to find the old foundations.

This was not the first time that they had been consulted on the ancient city of Babel. During the reign of Nebuchadnezzar's father, they had carefully scoped out the outer walls and the location of the inner ring of irrigation canals. This ring was to be the most precise in its placement, as it would provide for the exact position of the twelve masks, should they be unearthed. All were known to be nearby.

I had finally found time, and a surreptitious moment, to re-engage Moreck through the fire of the furnace. "The scroll that your man handed over to me was blank," I began in a low tone of voice. "There must be some secret to reveal its writing."

"Of course, but we did not want to send the code and the document together—lest they be intercepted. Just rub the juice of a lemon across the sheet, and it will resonate for you in due time."

I did as he instructed, and sure enough, by later that afternoon, the small scrape of parchment began to display an outline—faint at first, then fully visible with all the details needed to recreate the tower. This is exactly what the historians were trying to locate. I could only assume that it would be just a matter of time before they found these plans among their manuscripts too.

I was right.

Within two weeks' time, this drawing and others were presented before the king. He would restore the tower and complete the original builder's vision.

This project would take years to complete and change the look of the palace forever; nevertheless, it was begun on the full moon of the first harvest season. The great gardens of the private palace grounds were cleared, the ruins of the original tower supports were uncovered, and the foundations were rebuilt.

The architects and builders met daily with the king. As for me, I tried to carry on in seclusion as best I could.

The tower, once complete, would rise a thousand feet into the air, but it would be nothing without the placement of the twelve masks—and five of them were still missing.

In time, however, Nebuchadnezzar chose me to work directly with all the other seers in finding the missing masks, while the ones that we had were moved carefully into their likely homes around the circle.

The mask encircled by fire was indeed problematic. Not only was it located in a cave deep underground; it could not be approached. Any creature coming near the mask would be swept inside.

To remedy this special problem, the great stone movers were called in. They knew the ancient secrets of lifting objects with their minds—they would not have to come near the mask.

It took fifteen masters fully two months in order to move the mask to its finally resting place. This mask was the pearl of them all and rested at the most northern point of the circle—precisely why it had been so well hidden.

With a multitude of seers reporting directly to me, the Ma-ji could not hide their secrets for long. The seven known masks had been pulled immediately from their hiding places and arranged along the inner circle.

A poem written long ago presumed to tell where each mask should go, but one part of the script was worn away. It told only the names of the last two masks; lost were their positions on the ring. We would have to place them all before we would know where to set the last two—and we could still get it wrong, just like the first builders did.

It was at this time that the girl, hands clasped around a basin, began appearing to me almost nightly in my dreams. She would release the basin, which would float in midair, take my hand, and lead me over a hill into a blinding light, or she would lead me into the depths of a dense forest, or out through a grassy plain.

"Five there are that still remain, all to be raised and set up again. Man will profit from the twelve, into the darkness of his soul to delve. Respect the whole, let your ego decrease, and you shall live your days in peace."

Riddles. They have their place mainly because they are easy to remember, if not so easy to understand.

Like with most of my dreams, I did not presume to grasp the whole image on my own. I talked with the other seers, and slowly the pieces began to come together.

As more of the masks were found, the ones remaining became more anxious, longing to be discovered and reunited with the others. This translated into more intense dreams. We had seers, being called by the stone masks, arising in the middle of the night and journeying to where the masks were hidden.

In just a few short years, eleven masks had been found—all save one. Its name was "Oneness," a fitting name for the mask that would now unite them all. Without it, well, there was no without it; we had to find the last piece of the puzzle.

But it seemed that the well of dreams had dried up. The other seers were baffled by their blindness concerning this last mask's location. I, however, was still not completely alone in this endeavor; the girl of the basin still came, although not as regularly.

Moreck had refused to help in restoring the last mask, fearing that it might not be the time to try again to unleash their magic. I understood his concern, but felt compelled to push forward. Where was that last mask?

That night, the girl finally spoke again. "Answers are found within the right questions," she recited, as if talking into the basin itself. "All things can be known to those who are ready to receive the knowledge."

In the dream, I asked how I might know, how I might become ready to know. She told of eleven keys that, when held together, will open a twelfth door. The eleven keys are the eleven masks. "That which is found within them will guide the true of heart to that which is not found through reason's rhyme."

"So what you are saying is I have to solve the eleven riddles hidden within the masks in order to acquire the secret about the location of the last mask," I surmised.

"Yes. The many can only stand when sustained by the allegiance of the one."

The dream faded, but my mind could not let it go. I remembered everything and enlisted the help of my three best friends: e-Shack, Hanan, and Abed.

Since entering the adult world of real problems, we each had been tested and our resolve refined. Our collective experience would be invaluable in fulfilling this quest. First, e-Shack would be able to help me in understanding the political arena surrounding the coming together of the twelve masks of stone. Second, Hanan would be able to reach beyond logic with me, in order to unveil the meaning of the riddles. And finally, Abed, now a master in alchemy, would be able to hear the words of the wind, and be the eyes of the trees for me.

We banded together as never before and called upon the power of the four corners of the earth to help us. This was, in fact, our first clue—the four corners. We set about to identify ourselves individually with a unique location on the ring: north, south, east, and west. From these different perspectives, we could then work toward each other in completing the ring.

We cast lots to determine our points on the ring. e-Shack became the northern star of Babylon; Hanan was chosen as the westernmost light; Abed assumed the guardianship of the south; and I was designated as the eastern Ma-ji.

Hanan had designed a large tile floor that would accurately depict all the points on the ring and line them up with the astral plane. Quickly, workmen installed this model in a large outside courtyard close to our place of abode—we needed the stars and the sun over this spot.

A single universal, unifying force began to minister to us every night as the sun would set. We four would gather in our positions every day just prior to dusk and share the information that had come to us during that day.

Two scribes sat outside the ring and wrote down every word that was uttered. Our first task was to reveal the riddle of the north. We placed a large basin in the center of the tile circle and built in it each night an immense, roaring flame. The light would dance and sway, its fingers reaching into the air, grasping and releasing.

The soft glow was mesmerizing, lending itself to visions. Hanan had taken to physically examining the northern mask. He fashioned a replica of the stone image and brought it to each of us to examine. He also noted an inscription—gone unnoticed due to the intensity of the flame that constantly encircled this particular mask. A parchment displayed the scribbled outlines of an ancient writing and his attempt at deciphering it.

"In the north you find a star, to guide you through the muck and mire; but it is the light you cannot see that leads the heart and sets it free."

"Are you sure that you have translated it correctly?" I asked as I carefully weighed the verse.

"As best I know how," Hanan related. "It is difficult to make out some of the letters, but since I cannot pass through the flame boundary protecting the stone—to physically exam it—this will have to do."

"Well, then, ten more riddles to go. Maybe they will expose more of their hidden meanings once we situate them together. We will each take the two masks to our right, plus the mask position that we now occupy along the central lines of the ring, and copy down the ancient letters. We will then give them to Hanan to decipher." I had given my directive but felt uneasy about the next step.

As the weeks passed, the words of all eleven masks—and a hint of the twelfth—were compiled. From the great northern mask, engulfed in its protective flame eastward, the masks read thus:

> The Mask of Life Unending: In the north you find a star, to guide you through the muck and mire; but it is the light you cannot see, that leads the heart and sets it free.

> The Mask of Despair: When you've known the deepest night, you'll chance upon the brightest light.

The Mask of Innocence: Recognize what before your eyes is and see much more then delight and bliss.

The Mask of Separateness: In the illusion of one's self, find the connection to everything else.

The Mask of Honor: Honor the heart above the mind, and you'll know the unknown reaches of time.

The Mask of Truth: Truth, when twisted to deceive, scatters truth's abandoned seed.

The Mask of Endurance: Hearty souls continue on, long after mortal life is gone.

The Mask of Healing: A touch, a word, kind fellowship stirred, can heal the most untenable illness heard.

The Mask of Giving: From the heart the soul doth leap, to slow the pain that into minds doth creep.

The Mask of Oneness (although lost, an ancient tablet provided us this script): There is but one, and one there is. The many are broken; the remedy 'tis found in unity of all the shards into a single poem that binds the bards.

The Mask of Kinship: All are one and one is all; none are strangers upon whom we call.

The Mask of Hunger: We take that which we do not own, and leave the rest to suffer and moan. Fulfill your hunger from within, and reap life's benefits times ten.

Words of old had spoken once more, light cast upon a blind eye with wisdom to befuddle the soul. It was now our turn, like the ancients, to try to mend the broken pieces of human dissolution.

All masks had been identified and their mysteries opened. We embraced the poem which bards and minstrels had heralded throughout time. Now to find the last mask.

CHAPTER 13

Accepting the Dream Child

The netherworld of starlight and darkness—a gift to some, a nightmare to others—has reached out to me my whole life. And before I understood its great power, I, like so many others, feared my nightly journey.

Then my father told me about "guardians of the dream time." "They are always there to help and protect you; just call, and they will come in whatever form is needed to overcome the shadows. Fear is a choice you do not have to make," he used to always say.

For years, my father told me a bedtime story that I never really heard until I was much older and his face no longer graced my daily chores. He would put me to bed inside a cozy loft niche just above the fireplace—it wasn't very big, but it was all my own. It was always warm there, even on the chilliest desert nights.

Close your eyes, he would start . . . the palace is bright with torches around every corner. The marble glistens and the colorful weavings lend depth to the walls. Your every need is cared for—food, the finest attire, the most refreshing liquids, and the comfort of loved ones.

As he spoke, I would sink contentedly into a mattress of straw as if it were made of the finest silk and stuffed with goose feathers.

Every day, you play in the sunshine; every night, you bathe in the warmest of baths and retire to a golden bed piled high with pillows. Then one night, you cannot sleep. You are fearful that someone will come in the middle of the night and take you away from all the comforts that you love.

Mysteriously, the lights go out and a most frightening darkness fills your room. You try to call out, but even your voice has been scared away. You cower under the sheets, afraid to look out. Just then, it happens—at this point in the story, Father would grab the covers and rip them from my tight grip—men dressed all in black surround the bed and pull you from it. They carry you deep into the desert, only the night stars guiding the way.

They spy a small village in the distance; grain fields scattered all around. It is here that they put you down. Scared and alone, you make your bed amongst the wheat and cry yourself to sleep. In that sleep, you dream of a girl—innocent and untouched by such tragedy—who grasps your hand and takes you to the top of a distant hill. Together you overlook the ruins of a faraway city—smoke rises high into the air and flames rage upon that place.

"Only you have survived," the girl explains. "All others have been killed by a fierce band of criminals intent upon having your gold. Do not try to return, and seek not revenge. Stay in this village; love them with all your soul as they, in turn, will love you."

"But . . . my family . . . what of my family?" the small boy cried.

"Never fear, for they are with you always," she comforted. Then she added a most strange pledge. "On this day we give you a gift—not just to you alone, but to all your sons after you. From this day forward, you shall be able to see the world more clearly through your dreams than through mortal eyes." And before she vanished from the boy's dream, she handed him this and said, "Keep it under your pillow, it will remind you of what once was, and you will know the sagacity of the dreams that come to you in the night."

That young man grew up right here in this very village and had a son, and that son had a son. And he never knew that he was, in fact, a prince.

Father would then pull a small bit of brilliantly colored cloth from underneath my pillow—he had given it to me upon the first telling of this tragic story.

This was all that was left of the multicolored coat that the prince once owned, he would say in a sad voice, and now it is yours.

He would tell me that I was heir to a vast kingdom of immense wealth and power. I would always fall asleep to that story. I loved it so much that years later I would have my father fashion a small medallion so that the cloth could be placed inside and always worn about my neck.

I have since learned that the boy prince was none other than my grandfather, and my gift of second sight comes through him. I have also come to believe that the girl of the basin is the same girl that once melted the fear in my grandfather's heart on the very night he was carried away from the shattered palace.

The king had begun to grow impatient with the efforts to find the last mask. In my dreams, I wandered about aimlessly, seeing much but finding nothing but disappointment. It was then that I remembered my father's words: Dream guardians are always there to help you; just call.

So I called, and she, the girl of the basin, answered.

"Do not be saddened by your long journey to find the last mask. You have always been on the right path. And now it is time to see the oneness of life . . ." She pointed at the very spot where Wildfire and I spent many a secluded evening in quiet meditation. "It has been there beneath your feet all the time," she let me know as she faded before my eyes. "Go quickly. Others seek to usurp your claim to the last mask."

When I awoke, it was still dark. I dressed and bolted from the room.

My first stop was Arioch's quarters. Now it was my turn to rouse him out of a sound sleep.

"Come quickly," I called. "I know where the last mask is hidden, but it won't be hidden for long; others are even now on their way to steal it out from under us."

CHAPTER 14

The Last Mask Is Lost

Frantically, we rushed from the palace. Arioch went to gather several other guards to assist us. He—knowing the spot as well as I—tarried in order to made preparations for the return of the mask once we had it; while I, on the back of Wildfire, wasted no time in attaining the location.

As Wildfire and I rode swiftly toward our destination, I became aware of just how much I had missed my daily excursions with him. I had become so busy since leaving school behind it seemed that I had left him behind too. I promised myself at that moment to put my priorities where they rightly belonged.

I scanned the distance, looking for any sign of others. This was a remote spot, and human intrusion would be evident even from a great distance. While my eyes roamed the horizon, my heart began to sink—a mountain of soil disfigured the otherwise pristine plains.

We were too late!

Arioch and fifteen palace guards arrived only a short time later. Tracks gave ample clues as to the direction that the bandits took. Arioch and his horde headed out to ascertain where they might lead.

I remained behind to sort through what I could of the earthen remains. There were broken pots and remnants of clay tablets, what looked like human bones, and something else—a sense that I was not alone, a celestial presence did indeed hang over this place. I had felt it before during my many jaunts to this sacred sanctuary of mine, but never so strongly.

The wound in the earth, the exposure of the last mask—they both had caused the spirit of time to weep. I fell to my knees then and there, and a vision came upon me.

"Do not be blinded by your double vision. Where you see two and think that there is but the one, see one doubled as two. Identical twins they are, but with different souls. Read the writing and know the difference" was the message that she repeated over and over again.

I soon awoke. Wildfire and I waited for the return of Arioch to learn the fate of the last mask. The sun was beginning to set, and the nearby stream reflected its golden fury into my eyes. Tears for the loss of all that we had battled for over the last several years ran down my face.

Still far afield but steadily approaching, the thunder under my feet told me that Arioch would soon be arriving with his troop. I cleared my thoughts, remounted Wildfire, and waited for the report.

"We followed them to the main road, but the wheels of the cart have vanished. We will send word throughout the kingdom tonight. Maybe someone somewhere saw something; but this is such a remote part of the kingdom, I do not hold out much hope. But a mask of that size is not going to be easy to conceal. We'll find it sooner or later." His report finished, Arioch and the fifteen exhausted and hungry guardsmen rode away. I trailed listlessly behind, thinking.

Once back at the palace, I gathered the band of four together and recounted every word of the vision.

"Double . . ." Hanan mused. "Something in one of the older scrolls mentions two—these twins that you speak of— but the rest of the parchment has been torn away . . . go figure! It is useless. I have searched long already to try and recover that part of the writing."

Abed had a look of bewilderment in his eyes. Then, like pieces of a puzzle falling together, a glimmer of recognition washed over him.

"In nature, many things look alike: leaves, blades of grass, even trees. But all things are as individual as you or me. Just because they look the same does not make them the same."

"Uh-hum," I sighed. "And this helps us—How?"

Quiet up to that point, e-Shack now chimed in. "Double vision . . . that's the key. Daniel, when you know what that means, your eyes will be opened and you will find the last mask. You are the seer, and in due time, you will see that which others do not . . . in a place that others fail to notice. You alone have the gift of blind sight."

He spoke in an almost prophetic way, bringing a hush to the entire room. Silently, we each broke away to our separate quarters. Why me? So many others are more skilled, more tenacious in their studies, more practiced in their art.

I fell asleep questioning the mettle of my own heart. "Do not concern yourself with the 'why' or the 'how' of life. Seek only to follow the path—your path. The mind will never be able to answer the questions of the heart."

One voice in the night had quelled a lifetime of self-doubt.

The morning brought fresh news. Arioch sprang through the doorway, extreme anguish falling from his face. "We found the cart, but no sign of the mask. It seems that everyone has seen a mask at some point over the last several days, but the descriptions match all the masks that we already have.

"We have posted extra men around all the standing sites, just to ensure that no other masks mysteriously go missing," Arioch continued. "The king wishes to see you. He is quite anxious over the apparent loss of the last and most important mask."

"I know. I've been expecting his call."

Arioch shrugged his shoulders and left the room. "Don't keep him waiting too long. It will just be worse for you when you finally do arrive," he yelled from outside the door as he strode away.

I knew that all too well, but that is not what was stopping me from seeing him straight away. What would I say? I was in a tight spot and I don't mind admitting it. The king had a way of rewarding to the tenth degree those he favored; but those who displeased him, well, sometimes they just vanished.

All too quickly, I had arrived at the king's council chambers. He was sitting quietly at a very large table, scrolls and tablets strewn about it. He glanced up only briefly upon my entrance into the chamber, and then reaffixed his concentration upon his review.

With his head still down, he began to speak, "I read here that you have been unable to complete the uncovering of the last mask. Someone seems to have beaten you to it."

"Sir, I can explain . . ."

"I am confident that you can," his eyes finally meeting mine. "I am sure that I do not need to remind you, of all people, that the welfare of the entire kingdom rests on our being successful in restoring all the masks. I will await your good word once you have rectified the situation. Do not disappoint me in this matter—"

I was dismissed after saying only four words. The king was a man of action and not one for excuses. He was right, of course. Instead of spending my energies trying to come up with a plausible explanation, I needed to redirect my attentions to finding the last mask.

Dejected and rebuffed, I wandered about the palace trying to come up with a plan. Then it hit me—Moreck . . . the furnace. Maybe he knows what has happened.

I made my way to the furnace, doubling back many times in case I was being shadowed. "Is anyone there? Moreck?" I listened but heard only the flames crackling roar.

Then someone called, "Who's there?"

"It is Daniel. Is Moreck around?" Silence. "Is Moreck there?" I repeated urgently.

"I . . . huh . . . I will get Barthalemu for you. Wait there," he answered awkwardly before running off.

Strange, Moreck had always been around to assist in critical times like these. He must know about the theft of the last mask—the whole kingdom knew at this point.

Within a few minutes, Barthalemu called to me through the flame, "Are you well, Daniel?"

"For the moment, yes. Where is Moreck?" I asked directly.

"He, well . . . we don't know where he is. He disappeared a few days ago, and we have had no contact."

"You don't think that this has anything to do with the last mask, do you?" Barthalemu was well aware of the rift between Moreck and me over restoring all the masks and completing the circle.

"Actually, we do. I have always suspected that his aspirations were not in line with ours. Watch yourself. I do not know the extents to which he will go to stop the reunification. He knows that you alone have the insight to fulfill the prophecy."

"Prophecy . . . what prophecy?"

"Your prophecy. I should have told you all this before now, but you were young and . . . well . . . we didn't, and that is that. The short version is this: Ancient manuscripts have long told the tale of a great kingdom that would rise from the dust of Babel. The great tower would soar into the heavens once again, but not on its own. There would be one who would come—from a distant land—and unravel the riddle of the twelve masks. You will know him by his ability to interpret dreams, and most importantly, you will know him as the only one able to enter the fire of the northern mask and return with whatever he holds in his hands. That person, my friend, is none other than you."

"Was that just a test when I rescued the two of you from the fire?"

"Not from me, I assure you. Moreck had sent one of his own into the flame, believing that you would be able to save him and verify the prophecy. Upon finding out what he had done—risking an innocent life in order to prove the prophecy—I tried to perform the rescue myself, and in turn, was caught up into the flame as well.

"But I never had a doubt that you couldn't save us. I was, however, unsure of your willingness and courage in the face of what might have meant certain death for us all."

"I . . . had . . . no idea . . . what I was . . . doing . . ." I stammered.

"You didn't have to. You only had to step out with confidence. Doors will always open for you, but only when you are in the right place at the right time. Not knowing any of that, you still did the honorable thing. It was a very proud moment for all the remaining Ma-ji." Barthalemu's words left me mute. "Now back to the issue of the last mask," he said. "We have seen in dreams two masks that look the same . . ."

"Twins," I said, thinking aloud in retrospect. "We have seen them too."

"Exactly! We believe that the twins represent the masks of separateness and oneness. We will continue to search the ancient documents for any more clues. As for Moreck, we'll let you know when we locate him. Again, be careful!"

When I arrived back at our quarters, only e-Shack was to be found. "Where is everyone else?" I asked, concerned that another major crisis had arisen. It was very late.

"Oh, Hanan had a flash of insight or something, grabbed Abed, and ran out. They said they would be back soon and explain everything."

"What is wrong with you? You don't look so well," I observed.

"Probably something I ate. Now that you've mentioned it, I am very tired. I believe that I will go up to bed. If you don't mind, we will talk tomorrow." And e-Shack pushed aside the mounds of work cluttering his desk and staggered upstairs.

Just then, Hanan and Abed came running back in. "We have found out more about the twins," Hanan started in.

"Yes, the ancients were very good at hiding their secrets. You won't believe what they did," Abed added.

Hanan threw down the scrolls that he had clinched precariously under his arm and began to pore through one then another.

"What are you looking for?" I finally asked.

"Here it is," said Hanan.

> Power has no will of its own. It can only magnify the will of others—both the good and the bad. In the hands of benevolence, a veritable garden of Eden will once again bloom; but in the hands of malice . . . domination, slavery, want, and death will prevail. Be hereby warned that even the most caring of hearts can be swayed to evil by such might. Therefore, as a final guard against the misuse of this power, two masks have been bound together in spirit. Neither mask will function without the

recognition of their unity . . . that recognition can
only be transmuted via a single crystal which has
been divided between the two. If the one who divides
the crystal is impure, that soul will perish . . . you
have been warned.

"And there is something else," Abed added, "uh . . . in
this scroll: 'The crystal can only be broken in the middle—
its parts separated evenly.' I don't know what that means.

"Where is e-Shack? He should hear this too," Abed
queried.

"He wasn't looking well when I came in. He went up
to bed," I said.

"I'll go check on him!" In short order, Abed bolted up
the stairs, anxious to be the first to fill e-Shack in on the
latest findings.

A frantic shout came from the top of the stairs, "Daniel,
Hanan, come quick!"

We found out e-Shack had not made it to the bed. He
lay in a heap on the floor, drenched in sweat and
unconscious. The three of us got him quickly up, peeled off
what clothes we could, and settled him in. Hanan went
immediately out to summon the royal healers. Abed and I
did what we could with cold water and damp head
dressings in an attempt to reduce the fever.

When the healers finally arrived, they shepherded us
from the room so that they could perform their magic. Hours
passed with nary a word, while others were called in by
the healers. But a worried look shrouded each face as they
sidled quickly past us out of the bedchambers. None would
even meet our eyes, and all—save the most senior of the
healers—refused to tell us what was happening.

"We wanted to be absolutely sure before we gave you
our diagnosis. Your friend has been poisoned by a highly
complex and aggressive substance. We will, of course, do

what we can . . . but recovery from this type of malady is extremely rare."

We all sat stunned at the thought that such a thing could have happened so quickly.

"He was fine just a few hours ago . . . we . . . we were laughing about the . . . the . . ." Abed's words had deteriorated into garbled murmurings through his tears.

"Hanan," I had pulled him aside, "take care of Abed. I am going to find out if the Ma-ji knows of any way to help. It appears that we don't have much time."

I ran from the room and set my path as directly as I could toward the furnace. As I ran, however, a strange foreboding filled my heart—something or someone was stalking me, shadowing my every move.

Stopping dead in my tracks, I did not even bother to turn around. I could feel the icy breath of doom, and then I could hear the faint rattle of its words: "They won't be able to save him; time will run out on your dear friend's mortal life. Only you have the gift that allows entrance into the northern mask. The fruit of eternal life still grows within. Nothing less than that will save him."

"Why do you care about my friend's life?" I knew that there had to be a catch. I just didn't know what it was yet. "Let's get Barthalemu or others in the Ma-ji to help."

"There isn't time. We must go alone . . . I will pull you back through the flame. Run, or you will miss your chance. I will meet you there."

The presence was gone, but the words it had spoken rang true. I had no time to enlist the help of others, so I caught the first barge to the northern city and arrived at the mask several hours later. It was still dark and the flames were more blinding than ever.

As I stared into the swirling mass, the voice once again chilled my spine. "Don't turn around. Tie this rope around your waist and walk into the flame—like before."

I did as he said, but as I walked forward, two words echoed loudly in my ears—like before. The flame swept me up into its vortex once again. This time, however, I was able to make my way across the flaming divide into a calm eye where stood the great mask of the north.

My feet now back on firm ground, I tugged for more rope and made for the mouth of the stone monolith. It looked completely solid; but as I approached, the mouth opened, and a brightness to pale the flames surrounding me, dazzled my senses.

Once inside, multicolored stars engulfed me, flowing through me as well as around me. I reached out to touch one, and it lighted softly on my hand. "Plant the seed beneath your feet and you shall have what you came for." No audible voice spoke, but I did as instructed.

The ground under me was as black as pitch. I placed the seed there and covered it gently. A low rumble began to shake the entire mask, and as I jumped back, I watched life spring up in an instant—branches, leaves, blooms of the sweetest fragrance, and finally, fruit. It was translucent and reflected the light of the stars.

A single piece of fruit hung just within my grasp. I did not want to rip it from the branch, but a sudden quick tug on my rope told me that it was past time to go. I grabbed the fruit and watched the tree wither and dissolve back into the ground.

My body was once again caught up inside the flame's grip. It seemed more reluctant than ever to let me go. Just when I thought that the rope might actually snap, I was thrown free and landed at the feet of a man, a man that I knew well, or at least thought I did—Moreck.

"You . . . what have you done?" I blurted out once I had regained my speech.

"For a seer, you do have some pretty convenient blind spots," he began. "Barthalemu was starting to suspect me a little, but you always seemed to believe everything that I said."

"Barthalemu has already told me that it was you who set up the first test with the flaming swords. You knew the prophecy, didn't you? And you were willing to bet someone else's life that I was the one. What if you were wrong? Barthalemu risked his life to bail you out."

"Oh, don't get so high and mighty. You, sitting at the right hand of the king, eating sumptuous meals every day while I languished away in that dark, damp cave. I have lost my family, I lost my business, and I lost my pride. My name used to mean something in this kingdom . . . no more. Then you come along, a child from some second-rate farming community. You're the one who is going to set everything right."

He continued his rant: "Who do you think saved your good-for-nothing grandfather from the bandits? That's right. It was my small band of the Ma-ji, stationed out in that remote, pitiless part of the world. You wouldn't even be here now if it weren't for us. As such, I believe that I am entitled to a little bit of something in return.

"And if you don't mind, I'll take that fruit that you have in your hand."

"You think that you are going to eat this and live forever? Not as long as I am alive to stop you," I shot back.

"Admirable! But I, being a Ma-ji, descendent of the ages, know all too well the limitations of mortality. I have no such wish. But the king, on the other hand . . . He will reward me handsomely for bringing him this. And with the last mask still lost—is it? You, I imagine, will just disappear from the face of the earth."

"It was you. You poisoned e-Shack, didn't you? You knew that I would do anything to save my friend."

"Too bad you are not going to make it in time!" His eyes for the first time left mine to gaze longingly at the fruit I was still clutching in my hand. I instinctively looked down at the fruit too, but it did not look the same—it was decaying.

"Moreck, you can't give this to the king. It is . . ." All I remember seeing was the rock that he had swung heavily at my head.

When I awoke, Barthalemu and his band were helping me to my feet. The fruit was gone, and so was all the hope of saving e-Shack's life. Then I thought, "Help me to go back in; I may still have time to save e-Shack."

Barthalemu held on to my arm tightly. Even through blurred vision, I could see that what he was about to say was bad news.

"Only once, once in a lifetime, can the chosen enter the mask of life unending. Moreck knew that well. I am sorry for your friend's life. If I knew of any other way to save him . . ." Barthalemu broke off as tears filled his eyes. "My two friends here will help you back to him. You need to spend what time you have left together. Go quickly!"

Still reeling from being hit by the stone, I would never have been able to see my way clearly to return to the palace and to our quarters without their help. They brought me as close to my destination as they dared go. I tottered up the final steps and met Hanan at the door.

"They don't give him much time. Abed is with him now. I take it that you weren't able to . . ."

"No. I held his life in my hand, but . . ." I wept as we ascended to the darkened bedchambers.

"We all know you did your best . . . we will leave you alone with him."

Hanan and Abed crept from the room and closed the door behind them. Darkness flooded my soul as I sat before the last glimmers of life lying on the bed in front of me.

"I am so sorry, my friend. One of my trusted guides at the Ma-ji has betrayed us. It was he that poisoned you in an attempt to force me to retrieve the fruit from the mask of life unending."

His near-lifeless body barely moved as he breathed a labored breath. The morning sun's rays were just beginning to filter through cracks in the closed shutters. Sensing his life slip away, I placed my fingers to my lips, kissed them, and touched them gently on his.

Exhausted, I laid my head on his chest and fell into a deep sleep. In my dream, a slowly dying flame appeared before me—not unlike the nightly fires we had known during our desert crossing on our way to this land. Within its burning embers, I could make out the darkened form of a man staring intently back at me.

I recognized the form right away; it was e-Shack. He spoke: "Your quest for the life of another has not been in vain, for you carried back more than just the fruit from the mask; you had the very juice upon your fingers. In touching your fingers to my lips, you have saved my life. But it will come back most slowly. You must not now tarry, however, for the king's life is in great jeopardy. You must stop him from eating the fruit. You must stop him from eating the fruit. You must stop him from . . ."

I awoke in a sweat. I noticed e-Shack was breathing normally now, and in his semiconscious state, he spoke, "Go, quickly. You must stop Moreck!"

At that moment, the door burst open. It was Abed. "I thought that I heard . . . oh, e-Shack, you're alive, but . . . but . . ."

"Take care of him," I yelled as I dashed from the room. "Hanan! Help Abed. I have to find the king."

I went to the palace council chamber, but the king was not there. "Where is the king?" I hastily demanded of the guards.

"The king left this morning for the southern city of Pandora. You will find him at his royal accommodations there."

Moreck already had a great lead over me. How was I to get there in time to stop him? I wondered. Then I remembered what day it was. This was the special Festival of the Maidens. The king would surely be there, for he never missed it—Moreck wouldn't know that.

I was able to flag down one of the specially designated palace water taxis. I was at the Pandora royal accommodation in just less than an hour. It was empty, as I had suspected. Jumping on the back of a passing cart, I headed out to the festival grounds. Racing to the king's box, sweating and out of breath, I excused myself and inquired about the king's current whereabouts.

"Oh you just missed him, my dear," his wife cooed. "He was called away on a very urgent meeting with a council member. I believe they are chatting in the palace refreshment tent out back."

"Thank you most kindly, my lady." I bowed lowly, trying not to appear to be in too much of a rush, then casually retreated from view. Once out of sight, I scrambled toward the tent. Would I make it in time?

The soldiers that stood guard at the tent's entrance delayed me for only an instant before bowing me into the room. Since I was so close to the king, I was permitted an audience at anytime—without being announced first.

I would like to tell you that I made it in time—like with e-Shack—but it was not to be. Moreck stood to one side, an air of revelry beaming from his face, as the king was just finishing the fruit.

"No, my lord, no. The fruit cannot be eaten once it has been removed from the mask." My winded speech was too late—Moreck had won. The king had what he had always most desired: an eternal reign for his eternal kingdom.

The king looked upon me with repugnance and disdain, much like he had when I was a young apprentice. He stood confident and erect, and with a most stately expression, sat down at a table. He began signing documents. I can only suppose that he was fulfilling his promise of wealth and status to Moreck.

I stood powerless to stop these events. Still panting and grasping at a stitch in my side, I looked again at the king that I had so trusted, a king that had so trusted me, but something was not quite right. As the fruit had begun to wither once it had been taken from the mask, so too did the king's features dissolve into chaos.

Helpless to stop it, Moreck and I watched as the king was reduced to nothing more than an animal. His eyes dimmed; his hair lengthened into course, stringy tangles; his fingers resembled the claws of a bird more than the hands of a man. Wasted, he fell to the floor. His lips moved, but no language proceeded from them—only beastly grunts and growls.

Moreck, fearing the worst, took off, leaving me to try to explain all this. I stuck my head through the flaps that made up the tent doors, careful not expose the mess within, and informed the guard that "the king kindly requests the queen's presence."

"Dear, you are missing the most important part of the festivities. What can possibly be so vital as to keep you away so . . . long . . ." her voice trailed off as she entered the tent and looked from me to the strange animal next to me, and back again. "Where is my husband?"

I simply pointed down at the poor wretched beast at my feet and grimaced.

"Not again."

"Again! You mean this has happened before—" shock ringing from my voice.

"Keep your voice down. The guards mustn't know. It would be all over the kingdom before morning, and where would I be then, pray tell me! So what was it this time? Another youth elixir or eternal life concoction, I suppose."

"Well . . . fruit from the mask of life unending. Moreck gave it to him."

"I'm impressed! He's been after that one for years—ever since a traveling bard filled his mind with ancient stories about a tree of eternal life lost somewhere in the foundations of Babel. I had hoped that it was all just a tall tale, but one thing about the king, if there is any truth in a matter, he will certainly find it and drive me crazy with it until his next obsession comes along."

The queen seemed to take this much better than I had anticipated. "We'll just have to wait for it to wear off, I suppose. Daniel, I will need you to run things while the king is . . . away. And whatever you do, do not let that band of barmy soothsayers find out, or the only thing any of us will be ruling over is a small caravan headed out of town."

"Yes, my lady. It will be done as you wish."

It wasn't easy, I can tell you that . . . getting the king back to the palace. But that was only the beginning of our troubles.

CHAPTER 15

The Bite of the Fruit

Hiding a king that now had more in common with a goat than a man had its problems. First of all, the king liked—no, he loved—to be seen. But something else worked in our favor—the king was very, very paranoid. He saw plots to kill him in the most ordinary duties.

One time, during the opening of a new public library, the regional governor went to hand him the sword to cut the ribbon. He swore for months after that the governor was part of a secret plot to kill him and take over his thrown.

The hardest part was keeping our stories straight. We told the public that he was off reviewing a war campaign in the west. We told his personal guards that the king had uncovered yet another plot to kill him, and they were to guard his double—yes, we found a double—as if it were him, to throw any villain off the trail.

Now the immediate palace staff was kept in the dark about the whole thing—except Kira, that is. It was she who cared for the daily needs of the king in hiding. She would make sure that he had plenty of green grass for grazing— he seemed particularly partial to clover. She would also ensure that he was kept clean. He was no longer allowed in the bedroom—he kept trying to eat the sheets—so a special pin was put up for him in the private king's garden just outside the bedchambers.

After a few weeks of this, I found myself growing concerned that King Nebuchadnezzar would never come back to his former self. I was actually surprised that the fruit hadn't killed him. But he seemed stable enough, and we could communicate on a very basic level.

I now lived in the king's front chambers—just to ensure that no one gained access without Kira or me being aware of it. When the councilmen would start to get a little antsy about not seeing the king for a while and burst into my quarters demanding to see him, the queen (on a special cue from me) would begin the most raucous of arguments with the king in abstention. Not hearing the king respond to such outbursts of the queen was never a problem—as he seldom got a word in edgewise anyhow. The councilmen understood his lack of response quite well.

Upon hearing all the clatter and throwing of furniture, they would cower from the room, apparently not wishing to embarrass the queen by letting her find out that she had been overheard.

Sure this bought us some time, but it was starting to wear a bit thin. We would have to produce the king for all to see. But how to do it without giving anyone a chance to look too closely?

As predicted, e-Shack had recovered fully from the poison that Moreck had slipped him, and he became my constant companion in the palace on issues of politics and law. We kept the many lawyers running in circles, too busy to concentrate on the king's whereabouts.

I found out that most people would avoid a direct meeting with the king if at all possible. Although fair, the king's countenance could fall in a heartbeat and deliver the most scathing of pronouncements.

I also began to notice how much e-Shack resembled the king—oh, not in the face so much, but in overall demeanor, and most importantly, in his stride as he marched about the palace grounds.

With just the right amount of kingly accessories, and a beard of course, e-Shack as king would let himself be seen there and about. Oh, never so closely so that someone could stop him and engage him in conversation, but close enough to alleviate most suspicions.

There is always one, though, that can never quite be convinced by such tomfoolery. This is usually the one with the biggest mouth and the most worthless position in the king's court—yep, you guessed it—the king's dresser.

The king was fastidious about his garments. They had to be perfect, and no matter how much attention was paid to making them so, they never quite measured up.

Like a barking dog in the night, the dresser's howl could be heard every morning as he was refused entry into the king's quarters.

"The king will have my head if his garments are not perfectly tailored, and his waistline changes almost daily . . . I must see him!" He would decry for all to hear.

Sure, I could pass a look-alike king off at a distance, but like a barber, the dresser cannot be fooled. So we brought him into our confidence—well, mostly. The queen and I informed him that the king had embarked upon a new diet and would be keen for an entirely updated wardrobe once he had attained his goal, but that he could not possibly see a mirror—or his dresser—until that time.

"But when would that time be?" he asked impatiently. Then, like an arrow shot into a bull's-eye, it hit him. "Did you say 'an entirely updated wardrobe' would be required once he, the king, has completed his diet?

"YES!" the queen and I answered in unison.

"Oh my, oh my . . . work to do . . . much work to do. Must go! Can't stay around here chatting all day, can we? If you will excuse me, my queen, Daniel . . ."

Finally, he was out of our hair—for a little while at least. Now back to the bite of the fruit. I was in constant communication with Barthalemu and my other friends at the Ma-ji. First, we had to find out what this was. Was it a poison? Was it a spell? Was it a curse? And most notably, did it require an antidote or just time?

Back to the books and back to the healers. This is where Hanan and Abed came to the rescue. Abed had read about potions that would turn an enemy into an animal-like creature, but finding the reverse was not much called for.

Hanan dug through a mountain of ancient texts looking for anything that mentioned the fabled Tree of Life. Had anyone ever been known to eat of it, and if so, what happened to him? Maybe they were still alive, or maybe they met the same fate as King Nebuchadnezzar.

This then became the common point between Hanan and Abed's research. If someone else had eaten of the fruit and fallen into the same state as the king now existed, there might be some prior record of treatment.

A historical records search turned into a medical records search, but to no avail. It was Abed who finally laid bare a truth buried inside a bard's tale—the missing piece. Rather coincidently, a traveling minstrel troop came to the palace on their way from the East, they said, but no one had ever heard of them before.

"Let me tell you a tale of the fruit of life," a wizened old chap began, "and of a bite once made that is given right back . . . teeth do grind and pulverize its flesh, but flesh, once immortal, stifles the soul and draws it back to the dawn of time, and the beast of mankind finds new wings.

"To undo the good that has turned out wrong, bring the subject to the mouth of the river of song. At dawn, eat the fruit of decay and return to the self that once you were."

I don't know where I was when all this was happening. I must have been watching the acrobatics or been mesmerized by the superb jugglers. Only Abed heard the story of the bard. I would have accused him of making it up, if it hadn't been such a wild story.

Now, we had a tale of the right malady, a solution to that malady, and another riddle. This is where Hanan stepped in again.

"I have heard of the river of song." Once again, it was a fabled place. The waters rushed so over the rocks that they appeared to sing. Location on a map—unknown. "Well, who would have believed us if we told them that we had found fruit from the Tree of Life?" Hanan reasoned out.

As the king knew all too well, most fables have some basis in fact. You must find that grain of truth, plant it in fertile soil, and see what it might yield. Our first mission— find the bard. But the troop had disappeared . . . well, almost. They had certainly left the palace grounds, but they were due to stop in Pandora before heading into Egypt. Abed and I tracked down that lead, while e-Shack and Hanan took care of the subterfuge still required at the palace.

We had arrived just in time to hear the same bard deliver—with uncharacteristic gusto—the same tall tale. When he delivered it at the palace, he was so unanimated that only Abed took the time to listen.

Once the bard had completed this riveting new telling and retreated from the limelight, Abed and I were waiting for him. We quickly grabbed him—before he had a chance to slip away on us once more—and began to interrogate him on the location of the river of song.

"Why ya asking me? I didn't write up that cockamamie story, ya know. Heard it from a traveler when I was a lad, I did. Punched it up a bit to amuse the crowd, that's all. Why's you botherin' a poor old bloke like me fer? Help! Help . . . guards." He screamed as he tore away from us.

"Not another dead end," Abed decried. "I would have thought that this was it for sure."

"Well, let's get back to the palace before we are left with having to explain why we are terrorizing feeble, old bards," I suggested.

But before we had reacquired the palace taxi, a hissing sound caught our attention.

"Pssst . . . psssst, hey yuz!"

He was dressed shabbily, kept his head down and face covered. "Yuz looking for the river of song, are ya? For a coin or two, I can tellza' what I knows." He looked suspiciously around and then pressed us once more. "Look, I don't 'alf all day, ya know. What'll it be?"

"All right, here's you something for your trouble. Now what's the message?" Abed had given him a tidy sum, which elicited a babbling of gratitude.

"All right, all right, all right . . . what is the message already?" Abed demanded, his patience running out.

"Well, my lords, I heard tell of an old woman needin' to find a cure for her son. Ya' see, he had been such a nice and gentle soul, then one day, he became like a wild animal—snarlin' and a-bitin' anyone who would come near him. She was told to take her son down to the place where the women folk did beat out their laundry. Wash him in the muddy waters to cleanse away the wild, and feed him from the mushrooms that grow only there along the shallows."

The man made to hasten away, and we still did not know where this place was. "But you haven't told us where it is?" I shouted after him.

"It is within the palace grounds itself, right under your very feet. Ask any woman where to beat out the clothes, and you will find it." The man had disappeared even before his last words had reached our ears.

With the utmost dispatch and an ever-thickening sense of doom, we heralded our transport and set off for the palace.

"We are running out of time. We are running out of time. We are running out of time," Abed kept murmuring to himself as our destination slowly—very slowly—came into view.

"Pull yourself together! We will get through this . . . somehow," I had murmured more to myself than to him.

Upon docking inside the palace grounds, we met a most anxious Hanan.

"Oh no, what now?" I said as I tried to keep my calm.

"The councilmen . . . and the dresser . . . and Arioch—they all want to see the king, now! They won't take no for an answer. And the more they sit in there and talk to each other, the more they are going to know that we have been stringing them along for weeks."

If we ever needed a foolproof plan, we needed one now. "Don't worry, guys. I have it all figured out!" I always said things like that at such times, even though I was more clueless than Hanan looked at the moment. Think. We need time. "All right, I've got it." I explained my plan to Hanan and Abed on the way up the palace steps. They ran off to put the details into action while I had to find a way to stall for more time.

Sheepishly, I entered the room, "Lords and ladies, please . . ." as they had all started shouting at the same time. "How may I assist you this fine day?" I asked in my most casual voice.

"You know very well HOW YOU CAN ASSIST US!" the chief soothsayer railed. "Where is he? Where is our king? Or maybe," he now turned to address the frenzied crowd, "maybe, you have conspired with the queen to do away with a king that you have lost favor with."

An uproar filled the outer chambers of the king's quarters. I thought I was surely done for. Just then, the queen burst through the private chamber doors.

Every eye turned and not another sound was spoken. She quickly picked up from my expression of complete horror that the game was up, but I saw something else, something unexpected staring back at me from her eyes.

"What is the meaning of all this noise?" the queen fumed. "The king will have your heads for disturbing his afternoon slumber." The forcefulness of her defense caught them by surprise, but they had heard the slumber excuse far too many times by now to be wowed by it any further.

"My most gracious queen," the chief soothsayer's silky voice entreated, "we are most concerned over the welfare of our great king, none of us having seen him these past few weeks. We have grown wary of many excuses. We would not want the good people of the realm to be duped by a maniacal plot"—his voice became increasingly harsh—"hatched within these very walls to snatch the kingdom—"

The chief had stopped dead in his advancing tirade. The king himself had appeared just behind the queen, eyes still drooping with sleep, and staggered toward the crowd.

"What is the blasted meaning of all this NOISE!" the king shouted defiantly. "I try to get five minutes of sleep after being up for days working my fool head off, and this is what I am awakened to? I am giving you all just ten seconds to clear out, or I will personally see every one of you thrown in the dungeon."

That room emptied faster than if someone had just yelled fire. All that remained after that veritable stampede was the queen, the king, myself, and of all people—Kira. She had been among the crowd trying to calm things down.

"Will someone please tell me what just happened here?" I pleaded. I looked at the king first, but I don't think he understood most of it himself. The queen merely gave me a half smile and glanced over at Kira.

We all had a sit-down while the story unraveled. Kira started by telling us how Hanan and Abed had come running into the king's bedchambers right as I was about to enter the fray. She knew the exact spot that the stranger had told us to look for—it was just under the palace gardens, underneath the very spot where the king's pin had been placed.

She led the king down to the waters herself, as she had been training him to follow her for the past several weeks. Leaving Hanan and Abed to do the rest, she joined the others in the great hall, making sure that she would be seen by the most important councilmen. This way there would be no suspicion of collusion between the staff and myself.

It worked like a charm, as they say, and the king was returned to normal.

"But where are Hanan and Abed?" I asked upon realizing that they were nowhere to be found.

"Whatever do you mean," the king responded, "they are in their quarters. Where else would they be?" With a wink and a smile, I knew that everything was all right between us once more.

"It is interesting how grazing off the land has a way of changing a man's attitude about life," he quipped before turning on his heels and heading back to the bedchambers. "Sheets, soft white sheets, oh the joy . . ." we heard him say to himself as the great doors slammed shut behind him.

I thanked the queen and could do no less than hug Kira for the way in which she had saved the day.

Once back in my regular chambers—I had not slept in my own bed for over a month—I too slumped beneath the covers of home and thanked the heavens for the simple comforts of soft white sheets.

CHAPTER 16

The Circle Is Complete

In all the recent confusion at the palace, I had almost forgotten about the last mask—we still hadn't found it. It was not like I had a sword to my throat ready to strike if it didn't turn up in the next hour. The king was most appreciative for the job that I had done for him while he was, shall we say—gone. Nevertheless, a mask was still missing, and more to the point, Moreck was the key to finding it. If I could just talk to him. Not that I had a prayer of changing his mind, but perhaps, he would unwittingly give away some clues.

Barthalemu and his group kept a constant vigil out for any word about Moreck's new hiding place. "He was always our best spy, you know, so if he doesn't want to be found, I seriously doubt that he will be."

Like a thief returning to the scene of a crime, however, Moreck was finally caught by his own morbid curiosity. For days, we had noticed a stealthy presence come and go around our quarters. Never something that could be identified or seen straight on—a phantom inhabiting only the shadows, a glimpse out of the corner of the eye.

Knowing this cat-and-mouse game from my early days with Sol, I laid a trap. With just the right bait, I hoped to confront Moreck and reconnect with his dubious mind-set.

Since he was still most interested in e-Shack's recovery, that unease is where we planned to hit him. I remember that the sun rose that day with soft, muted brilliance. As usual, e-Shack had thrown open his windows to the morning and was meditating silently in full view of anyone who might happen by. Abed was the lookout—he could spot movement in the underbrush below like the eye of a hawk in pursuit of its prey.

We didn't have to wait long. The signal down, e-Shack began to moan and wail. Hanan, hiding in the wings, misted him with water to give the appearance of severe fever.

At just the right time, Abed bust into his quarters and proclaimed loudly—very, very loudly—that e-Shack had relapsed into the dark grip of death's hand once more.

Okay, Abed had the tendency to be a bit of a ham, but he did make the most out of the meager script that we had given him.

We shuttered the windows on the small balcony and made as if we were returning e-Shack to his deathbed. Moreck would want to get closer, and when he did—SNAP—the trap would be sprung.

I cornered him on the balcony just outside the darkened interior of e-Shack's death chamber.

"So, here to work more of your magic?" I began delicately.

"Daniel! I didn't see you there."

"I guess not. How have you been?" I asked, trying to feign a pleasant conversation.

"Look, about e-Shack . . . I mean, I realize now that . . . that . . ."

"You realize what?" malice growing with my every word.

"I'm sorry, all right. It was wrong to do that."

"To just him or to anyone else in particular?" I continued pushing.

"Daniel," Moreck said, still beseeching, "if I could take it all back, I would. Things got out of hand."

"What have you done with the last mask?" I countered while he was still earnestly trying to find absolution for his deeds.

His countenance changed in an instant. "I told you I would not be a party to you and your three friends reviving the power of Babel. Civilization is not ready—not ready! Why do you need me anyway? Can't the great and powerful seer of ages figure this one out on his own?" Moreck sneered. "You can't see what is right under your very nose, can you? All that ability, and so much of it still lies wasted inside your own ego."

Moreck bounded from the balcony and was lost in a crowd of wall dwellers on a sightseeing excursion. Abed and e-Shack fell brusquely through the windows, their knees having finally given out while straining to hear our conversation.

Rubbing a minor bump that he had just sustained on his head, e-Shack was the first to speak up. "So, what about the mask? Anything?"

"It is like what he said before: it is hidden in plain view. Unfortunately, there is an awful lot of plain view to go through before we'll know anything else.

When is a clue not a clue? When it has already been handed to you. I must be looking right through it and not seeing any substance.

Later that afternoon, I tracked down Hanan in the library. He was still researching the markings on the stones and how the twelve masks were supposed to work together. He had discovered that in each of the masks, there was an indentation in the forehead, as if something had been removed. Faded and smeared though the ancient script was, he had learned that a brilliant shard once adorned this void. The shards were very important, but he didn't yet know why.

My thoughts lapsed back to Moreck. "Hanan, what did Moreck mean by those words? Have I become too high-minded to see the details?"

"No, Daniel. Your heart is where it needs to be. But—"

"But what?" I pressed him.

"The but is that you must look outside yourself to decipher this clue. This isn't a riddle to lead you along the path of certainty. This is pure logic, requiring the powers of reasonable deduction. Ask yourself, 'What are you missing? What is always common between twins?'

"Now if you don't mind, I have to get back to these tablets. The library will be closing soon." Hanan never did like being interrupted while elbow deep in a manuscript.

With nary another word, he buried his nose back into his work. "But it is still morning, the library doesn't close until . . ." I tried to interject. Ah, well, he had given me enough to think about.

What is common between twins? No one had ever put it to me that way before, or maybe they had, but I just didn't hear it that way. When I was young, there was a set of twins in our village. I remember that their favorite game was to switch places and see how long they could fool their friends. Their girlfriends usually found this to be quite annoying.

But masks aren't people. Yes, but people move masks, don't they? A flash of insight had rocketed through my brain. I made my way to the canals and boarded a ferry headed in the direction of the known twin—it sat firmly in the east.

There it was, as always, staring out toward the rising tower at the center of the kingdom. Its eyes, mouth, and expression still "set in stone." Nothing, absolutely nothing was different from the last time that I had seen it.

Of course . . . nothing was indeed different since the last time that I had seen it, for that was right after the loss of the final mask, when I first found out that this stone was its twin.

But maybe it was different since the last time that Hanan had examined it. Skeptical at how outlandish that sounded—I must have been out in the sun too long—I pulled out some parchment and began to copy down, as I had done several months before, the engraving emblazoned across the front bottom of the stone.

The symbols looked no different, but the strange language that they represented would not have made an obvious comparison unless placed directly next to the writing of the twin mask. Hurriedly, I scrawled the letters down on a piece of parchment and returned to the library to consult Hanan once again.

I don't think that he had moved a muscle since I left him that morning—still sitting, still raptly engaged in some minute detail in the upper right hand corner of the very same tablet.

"Hanan, I do hate to bother you—"

"Again! Are you still here?" he groaned in a most irritable pitch.

"Yes. No . . . I mean, I have already left, been to the mask twin in the east, and come back. I wonder if you could take a look at something . . . these symbols from the stone."

"We catalogued those long ago," he mumbled without even looking up.

"I know," I suddenly whispered, as several grunts from the other library patrons let me know, in no uncertain terms, that I was causing too much of a disturbance. "I have a hunch, though. Please."

"Fine. My concentration is still broken from the earlier time that you interrupted me anyway. What is it?"

Our eyes met for the first time during the conversation. "I know that you have catalogued all the writings, but that is the obvious thing—the obvious thing that we would overlook. Here, compare this to what you wrote down in your log."

You would think that we would have to go back to his room to get the log, but true to form, Hanan had the log with him. I wouldn't have been surprised if he even slept with it under his pillow at night.

"Let's see . . . let's see . . . ah, here it is, the eastern mask translation."

Hanan reviewed both the original text and the translation in his mind before turning to the parchment that I had laid impatiently to his left side. "See . . . see . . . it is exactly . . . wooo, not exactly the same. Are you sure you got this right?"

"Yes, I was very careful. But if you want to go look at it for yourself, be my guest."

"No, it is just that . . . see these characters here. They are for the mask of the west, not the one located in the east. It seems like to me that you have found the lost mask of the west, my dear boy. That's the good news."

He paused for what felt like an eternity before continuing. "That's the good news, but the bad news is we now appear to be missing the original mask of the east. Without it, we still cannot complete the circle."

"Ahhh . . ."

My disgusted reaction was met with more shushing from an increasingly perturbed library patronage. "All right, we're going," I hissed back at them.

Hanan and I made our way down the library steps, still musing over the gravity of what we had just learned. "This is what was meant by 'what is common between twins,'" I said, "you know—their propensity to play the switcharue. Moreck must have switched the masks that day. But that still doesn't explain what he did with the true mask of the east . . . unless . . .

"Wait a minute." I had stopped dead in my tracks, causing a library student to ram into me and pitch his heavy load down the remaining steps.

"Sorry, sorry," I said, but before I had completed helping him to retrieve all those scrolls, I knew what I had to do.

"Tell Arioch to meet me at the dig site where the mask of the west was stolen. I have an idea!" I bellowed back at Hanan as I sped off toward the stables.

"Why?"

"Just do it. And thanks for all your help. I owe you big time."

Wildfire greeted me with the same unconditional enthusiasm as always. It was so good to see him, to ascend his powerful form, and to speed off into the plains once more.

We rode as one. I, with the knowledge that the circle would soon be complete, felt more alive than I had ever felt in my life. We arrived at the gapping hole—the hole from where the mask of the west had supposedly been stolen. Everything still looked the same.

Arioch, and a full complement of guards, soon joined me—just as they had on that fateful day when the last mask had disappeared. "What's going on . . . why are we back here?"

"My dear friend, Arioch," I began, relishing the certainty of my logic, "the mask of the west was never stolen, it was merely re-hidden. The tracks that you and your men followed to the road did indeed carry the mask of the west from this site. But what you didn't know was that the mask of the west had been carried eastward and set up on the same exact site belonging to the mask of the east."

"Hold it, hold it, hold it. What are you going on about?" Arioch interrupted.

I probably wasn't explaining it very well. It was so confusingly simple—that was the beauty of it. "Ok, let me backtrack a little. The masks of the east and west are identical . . . identical twins, right?"

Arioch nodded.

"So what Moreck did," I continued, "was to arrive at this site before us, remove the mask of the west, and to hide it under our very noses—by placing it in the east. Since it looks like the mask of the east, no one noticed when he made the switch . . . only a few markings on the front are different. Do you follow me so far?"

"Yes. So while we were all out looking for the mask of the west, it was standing in plain view. I get that. But you still haven't explained what happened to the mask that it replaced—the mask of the east."

"That's the beauty of it, don't you see?"

"What?"

"All he did was swap the locations of the masks. So—"

"So if the mask of the west was swapped out with the mask of the east, then the mask of the east would have ended up . . ." Arioch smiled his most mischievous smile.

"Right here!" we both shouted in complete harmony.

"Exactly," I continued. "They were careful to use the very same cart tracks on the return trip. I think if you have your men dig under the mound of dirt on the edge of this tear in the earth, you will find the mask of the east, hidden, just as Moreck had said, right under our feet."

"Excellent work, most excellent work, Daniel. The king will be extremely satisfied at hearing it."

In short order, Arioch had recovered the mask of the east, returned it to its rightful position on the ring, and moved the mask of the west to its final home. The circle was now complete.

CHAPTER 17

The Star of Babylon Hangs in Midair

There was a great celebration at the palace after the last stone had finally been set. And a new hope for the future seized the imagination of the kingdom. Work on the tower had gone on full steam throughout the search for the twelve masks, and it was now nearly complete. No expense had been spared on this colossal monument to mankind's greatest achievement.

The statue was of a woman, standing upright, with the heel of the left foot slightly raised, as if preparing to take the next step. Her head was adorned with a twelve-pointed crown of pure gold and encrusted with many fine jewels.

Once completed, she would be the symbol of wisdom—large enough for the entire kingdom to view. Even travelers would be able to glimpse her from a great distance outside the city. She was named Sophia, for she would be the guiding star of mankind.

As the final touches were being added to the immense tower, the band of four set out to resolve the mystery of how it should all work. What was this power that the ring was to provide? We knew from the bards that the ring, once activated, would give rise to a new star—a daystar—and its light would guide the kingdom into a golden age of prosperity and peace.

This age, it was said, would last for a thousand years. Never again would war and strife rip apart the soul of humanity. Never again would famine and disease destroy lives. Never again would hope be oppressed and happiness thwarted.

Yeah, it sounded too good to be true, but many were the stories passed down through the ages that related such an expectation. It was what kept humanity going—to find a way to make life somehow better.

We gathered nightly around the fire in the center of the lesser ring Hanan had constructed to help us fit the whole thing together in our minds. As the fire burned, we would focus our thoughts on the task at hand. Now the masks were still powerless without the shards. We knew that fact most of all.

The ancient manuscripts made it clear that the crystal shards were indeed dangerous. As a matter of fact, their power would consume anyone that dared even touch them. Their exact location—in a vaultlike chamber deep underground—was well known. The main reason why the location had never been concealed was that so many had died trying to pilfer the chamber for profit. The rulers of the time didn't want anyone busting into it unaware, thinking it was just full of harmless tomb artifacts. So they made it very clear where the shards had been encased.

Since that time of great grief, a special compartment within the chamber had protected the resting place of the thirteen shards. It is completely devoid of light and sealed against robbers. For thousands of years, the chamber had remained undisturbed.

It just so happened that the Ma-ji knew it well, for they had been the guardians of the power of the shards for eons. Barthalemu offered to take me there himself. He explained that over the years, the Ma-ji had installed certain obstacles to ensure the continued rest of the stones until such time that they should be resurrected from their slumber.

I only hoped that he had been correctly informed as to what those obstacles were.

Well, believe it or not, the shards were not buried deep under the foundations of the ancient city of Babel. No, the ancients took greater caution when locating these stones. They were buried far away—within the mountains of a snowcapped range. And getting there was half the battle.

It would be a month-long journey just to reach the entrance at the summit. Barthalemu made discreet arrangements for the caravan that would be needed to sustain us on the long trip. After weeks of preparation, they set out in the dead of night. I was to join them later, a two-day ride east, at a remote village.

I informed the king and Arioch of my plans; they both understood the importance of keeping this trip low-key. No one wanted a ransom situation to come up, should bandits acquire the stones.

Arioch, nevertheless, insisted that two guards accompany me on the trip. Bodyguards he called them. "Wouldn't want anything to happen to you either, would we?" he quipped as we took our leave at sunrise the next morning. "Be safe. See you in two months' time. If not, I will send a legion out to find you!"

The going was relatively easy the first day—flat, even soil with little wind to kick up the dust. But day two . . . if it could go wrong, it did. Rain pelted us. We were mired down in mud and almost missed the rendezvous point. Well, actually, we did miss the rendezvous point. Fortunately, one of Barthalemu's scouts found us wandering around and guided us safely in.

From there it was uphill all the way—first the foothills, then the really hard climb began. The carts were left in a camp at the base of the foothills, to facilitate our return trip. All needed provisions were strapped on to horses, and we rode higher.

At first, the cooler air was quite nice, but it didn't take long for it to get downright cold. "Don't worry, once inside the cave opening, it will get warmer. Well, it will at least seem warmer compared to this," Barthalemu reassured me.

After weeks of travel, our goal finally came into view, and Barthalemu pointed it out in the distance. "See that crack . . . in the wall above the cliff? That is the only entrance that will access the chamber. From here, we go on foot."

So once again, the burden was shifted. We moved from horses to an even smaller team of men who would carry the supplies. We all pitched in and shouldered the extra weight.

"What are those two poles for?" I inquired, wondering why we might need such things. "We aren't going to have to walk across some chasm on them, are we?"

"No," Barthalemu chuckled, "they will be put through the rings on that wooden crate—a black box with four rings, one at each corner—to carry the stones back. With these stones, the trick is how to handle them, not where to find them."

I don't mind admitting that I am desperately afraid of heights. You know the kind—a small narrow path with a mountain on one side and certain death on the other.

The cliff edge, which made up the entrance to the cave, was almost more than I could bear. With my face set firmly on the back of the man in front of me and my eyes squinted closed as much as possible, I attained the blackness of the cave.

This was yet another point where we shifted the burdens, left a base camp, and set off lighter in the backsides and fewer in number. It was there that I left my two guards as well. Barthalemu did not want them knowing too much about the protections surrounding the chamber.

A day's journey inside and Barthalemu, his two men, and I sat down for one final rest. "Listen carefully, Daniel," Barthalemu's words were soft and soothing—his fatherly attempt to bolster my sagging confidence, "failure to heed my warnings could mean your life. First of all, know this: the traps that have been set are not physical, they are more perception . . . how a person sees things, not necessarily how they really are. Two people can look upon the same object but see it differently and react to it differently based upon who they are and what they value in life.

"No one can tell you how to react in that moment; that is why so many have died in this place. But I would not have brought you here if I thought that your eyes were still closed to the fullness of life." He smiled dimly. "That is all I can tell you. Now let's rest for a few hours and then go and retrieve the stones."

In the silent bowels of the earth, I felt my heart pounding. It was then that I remembered my father's words: fear is a choice. At that moment, I decided not to choose it but to leave it behind in the darkness.

"All right, let's go!" breathed Barthalemu, breaking the expectant calm.

From a cavernous span, we ducked our heads to enter a relatively small room. It was not at all similar to the caves that we had been trekking through over the past day or so. The walls were smooth and straight. Crafted columns and sculpted scenes embellished a circular space.

There were a total of four openings off this rotunda, including the one that we had just entered. We moved to the center and cast our eyes about to take in the full effect of the view.

"What do you see?" Barthalemu suddenly asked me.

"I see four identical openings. It would be easy to become confused and not remember the way out," I replied, thinking I was being a bit too simplistic in my analysis.

"Good. Most people never take notice of how different a path is going to look on the way out, as compared with how it looked on the way in. Knowing that, we can now mark this opening so as not to confuse it with another later."

He continued his lesson. "There are three paths, which would you take?"

"I would take the quarter path to the right."

"Why?"

"Most intruders, I suppose, would march straight ahead first, not wanting to veer right or left. And on the right is always the seat of power."

"Good analogy. You would be wrong, but a good way to judge things."

"So, which chamber holds the stones?" I countered timidly, not wanting anyone else to hear.

"They are there, straight ahead, just like you first thought. Again, the trap is not in trying to hide the stones, the trap is in giving the intruders more doors, more doors that surely will yield more treasure. It is the trap of greed, my friend. Works every time.

"Put these on," Barthalemu continued, handing me a pair of lambskin gloves. "You must not touch the stones with your bare hands, at least not yet. You will go in, retrieve the stones by placing each inside its own pouch, and return them to me. I will tie them securely and place them inside the black box.

"The vault room is circular, just like this one. You must retrieve the stones in complete darkness and bring them to me one at a time. Take this pouch, place the first stone deep inside it, and fold over the flap. No light can touch these stones."

I looked toward the opening, shook my head to confirm that I understood, and headed into that eternal night. Once inside, even the torch light burning just outside vanished. This chamber had been sealed to let no light cross its threshold.

Panic started to grip my heart. No, I thought, Sol taught me long ago not to rely too heavily on my eyesight. I took a few deep breaths, closed my eyes, and saw something that at first I couldn't believe—the stones.

Like stars on the darkest night, they glistened inside my mind. One sparkled a little more brightly than the others. That, I assumed, was their way of telling me which one to take first.

One by one I removed the stones from their tomb—each being placed in a special pouch given to me by Barthalemu. He remained in the center of the rotunda and carefully packed each covered stone inside the black box.

The last stone that I removed was the greatest—much larger and brighter than the rest, it was positioned in the exact center of the dark chamber. This was the Sophia stone.

The inside of the black box sparkled in the torch light. It was lined with pure gold, even inside the lid. Barthalemu took special care never to come in contact with the lining.

Once all the wrapped stones had been carefully stowed and the lid replaced and locked, Barthalemu called for his two sentry men. Each had a long wooden pole with golden tips. First, one pole, then the other was pushed through the rings attached to the unadorned black box. The two men, standing between the poles at either end, then raised the box in one accord and marched out of the rotunda back into the damp bleakness of the cave.

Barthalemu led the way, and I brought up the rear. We took much care to keep the box as level as possible. This doubled the amount of time it had taken us in entering. Soon, however, the bright lights of the outside world— blinding us as it reflected off the snow—welcomed us back.

Down we came: from the summit, into the foothills, and back to our original base camp—the remote village. It was here that we split up once again. I left first with my two guards. Barthalemu and his troop would leave later.

We planned to hook up three days hence to deal with placing the crystal shards inside the stone masks.

Hanan was the first to greet me upon my return. "I take it that all went well."

"Yes, we will have the stones inside the kingdom tomorrow. Have you found out any more about how they work?"

"Some. The smaller stones will go around and the largest stone will be placed at the top of the tower. It is written that an alignment must take place in order for the stones to fire. I am still working on that part."

"Let e-Shack and Abed know that I am well. I must make my report before the king. I will be back tonight." I headed out to find Arioch and to make my presence back in the kingdom known to King Nebuchadnezzar.

The king was most happy that no ill had befallen me during my journey. I informed him that we had the stones in safekeeping and would begin to place them around the ring within the week. He also had the architects brought in so that a full report about the tower could be given; the projected completion—within the month.

The next few weeks were a most busy time. The lesser stones were being placed at an average speed of one per day. There was no need to second-guess where the shards belonged as each was unique and would only fit the mask for which it had been intended. Although each shard's unique contours defined which mask should receive it, the shards intended for the mask of the twins were different— they were fused together as one. There was a clear outline defining where they should be separated, but no one knew for sure if they would separate along that fault line. If broken improperly, both halves could be destroyed.

"Only two that have been bonded together by death can separate the shard," Hanan read from a scroll. "I think that this means that only you and e-Shack have the bond to correctly separate the shard. There's more. 'Both hearts must be pure and free of malice . . . by the laying on of hands, healing for mankind can begin.'"

"Well, that sounds simple enough. When does it say that the shard can be separated?" I stated firmly and without further consideration.

"'It must be separated on the dark of the moon . . . ' I believe that we have one coming up in just a few days—no problem!" Hanan heaved a sighed. "I will outline the rest of the ritual and expect to see e-Shack and yourself at sundown two days from now."

With that detail taken care of, I concentrated on the Sophia stone. Getting it up to the top of the tower without breaking it would take some finesse. We decided that the safest way was to take it up from inside the statue and not risk long ropes and the wind that might affect it if we tried to heave it up the outside among the myriad forms and scaffolding.

Still wrapped in the pouch in which I myself had placed the stone, workmen carried it up the staircase that wound its way to the top of the tower. Every several landings, the two workmen would rest. After every tenth landing, the workmen were swapped out. We would take no unnecessary chances now.

The Sophia stone, once securely atop the tower, would be held in a specially constructed wooden frame to support it at the exact height required prior to the stones' firing.

As the tower neared completion, additional security was placed around it to protect against sabotage. Only a select group of the most trusted workmen now gained entrance.

As the sun descended into the night of the moonless sky, Hanan, e-Shack, and I met to finalize our plan. Hanan, reviewing the tablet, gave the instruction: "The ritual can take place only after midnight. The shard is to be brought to the center of the ring—I take that to mean the tower—

and there be separated by two of the same heart . . . you two."

"All right, so far so good. What else does it say?" e-Shack asked.

"Something about using your bare hands . . . pure of heart . . . and pulling against each other—not snapping the stone in two."

Midnight crept very slowly upon us. Time seemed to stall. At the darkest part of midnight, we began. Hanan, using the specially made lambskin gloves, took the shard from its pouch, placed it on a wooden stand at the precise center of the kingdom, and cleared the area for e-Shack and myself.

A circle, ten feet in diameter, had been drawn on the floor around the wooden stand. "What now?" I quipped, looking cautiously at Hanan.

"On my mark," Hanan answered, "you will both start toward the stone from opposite edges of the circle, you from the east, Daniel, and you, from the west, e-Shack. And this is the most important thing: you must touch the stone at exactly the same time . . . got it? I will count it out. Ready?"

"Sure, why not . . ." e-Shack's voice sounded unsure all of a sudden.

Our eyes locked—to ensure that we moved in tandem. And Hanan began the countdown.

"Ready? Begin . . . two, three, four, five, stop. Now, on three, touch the stone . . . one . . . two . . ."

"Wait!" e-Shack shouted, jarring me to the bone.

"What now?" I yelled back.

"You can't touch the stone."

"And why is that?" I responded in an aggravated voice.

"What was that phrase, Hanan . . . pure of heart with no malice?"

"Yes, why?" Hanan wondered.

"Daniel," e-Shack entreated, "how do you feel about Moreck . . . for what he tried to do to me?"

"I . . . I . . . hate him. What he did is unforgivable."

"Nothing is unforgivable, Daniel. What you now harbor in your heart will destroy you and us. Do you not know that you hate yourself by hating him? Hey, I'm the one he tried to kill, remember? I have more reason than you to hold malice in my heart toward him. If I can forgive him, so can you. So what will it be, my friend? Time is running out." e-Shack had me there. I had let anger ruin my joy. "You are right, my brother. As you have forgiven him, so also do I from this very minute." My heart was instantly freed from an encroachment that I had not even realized had taken hold.

"Are you two quite ready, now?"

We both jumped having forgotten that Hanan was still very much there, outside the circle.

"Sorry. Continue," I said trying to refocus my mind.

"Once again," Hanan relayed, "on the count of three— one, two, three . . ."

A strange power ran through my arm and warmed my body. With our eyes still locked, e-Shack and I gently pulled at the stone, and it fell apart.

"All right, turn and head toward your individual destinations. You must, I repeat, you must have the shards in place prior to the first blush of dawn. Is that clear? Well, what are you waiting for? Go!"

We each took off at a run. We would have to maneuver through the palace grounds and find the horses that were waiting to carry us to the cities of the east and west.

It was six sarons from the palace center to the walled cities, and we now had only about an hour before the first tinge of dawn caught up with us. I was on Wildfire, of course, and he reveled in the challenge.

I arrived with several minutes to spare and could only hope that e-Shack had done the same. I watched the darkness dissolve over the kingdom and the sun's first tender rays lighting softly upon the crown of Sophia. The world didn't stop, so I assumed that everything had gone equally as well on e-Shack's end.

Wildfire was exhausted, so we hopped a ferry for the ride home. He had come through for me again, and for that I was most grateful.

I rested for the next several days; working through the night was never one of my favorite things to do. Hanan and Abed continued to search for the very last, and most elusive piece, of the puzzle—how and when the power would be released.

"I've got it!" Abed barked as he exploded into our quarters sometime later.

"Don't do that," I implored as I fell out of my chair. I was not one for loud noises, especially when I was half-asleep.

"Sorry, but I know how to activate the stones!"

"You do not," Hanan corrected him harshly. "I have been looking for months and still haven't gotten that far. What makes you so confident that you've solved it?"

"Well, smarty, I keep my ears open as well as my eyes. Not every answer can be found in a scroll, you know."

Hanan rolled his eyes and sat back down again.

"A storyteller in Pandora tells me," Abed continued, "that the star of Babylon will float in midair on the first passing of the sun directly over the tower after all thirteen stones have been set. And I guess that happens, what . . . twice a year?"

"Yes," Hanan countered unenthusiastically, "that does indeed happen twice a year. And what reason do you have to believe this person, may I ask?"

"Question, questions, questions . . . why do you always try to pick apart everything that I say?" Abed was in a right fury now.

"Just because somebody says something doesn't make it true . . ."

"Yeah," Abed shot back, "and just because somebody has written it down doesn't make it true either."

"STOP!" e-Shack had just entered the room. "What is all this shouting?"

Both Hanan and Abed tried to explain at the same time. "Stop," e-Shack roared again. "One at a time, please."

After all the stories had been told, silence finally washed over our little huddle. "I think that there is some truth to this," e-Shack mused. "The vernal equinox is rapidly approaching. If the stones fire, a new age will indeed begin."

He said it in such a matter-of-fact way that the ramifications of what was said took several minutes to sink in. A new age. None of us really knew what that meant.

We informed the king, and a countdown began throughout the kingdom. Fear gripped some, excitement others, and financial institutions were in utter disarray over the uncertainty. This prompted the king to freeze all assets and transactions until after the equinox.

The days ticked by more slowly than ever. At last, the final night before the vernal equinox had come. Thousands left the city in panic, while others decried the "end of the world." Still, with double guards around every stone mask, we held firm.

Days had become hours, and hours had become minutes. Just five more minutes to go before we would all know if this whole thing was real, or if it was just a fable— like so many other bard's tales.

At exactly midday, a flash of light shattered the calm. Its blinding light caused an immediate outcry, a pleading with the gods for mercy. Once the dread had cleared, however, oohs and aahs were heard from every corner of the kingdom.

The mighty sun's power had been refracted through the Sophia stone and rebounded from the lesser stones. This had the effect of boosting the energy to an unimaginable degree. The Sophia stone had vaporized the wooden scaffolding and now hung in midair above the great monument to wisdom. Its surface emitted a delicate glow. A new star had been born—a daystar. No longer fearful, the people began a celebration that would last for nearly a month.

The power that this daystar held is still a mystery to me this very day. But from that time forward, the kingdom prospered. Peace won out over war, and compassion ruled the hearts of men. Many were the ways through which the kingdom prospered . . . but that is another story.